Praise for Warren Adler's Fiction

"Warren Adler writes with skill and a sense of scene."
— *The New York Times Book Review* on
The War of the Roses

"Engrossing, gripping, absorbing… written by a superb
storyteller. Adler's pen uses brisk, descriptive strokes that
are enviable and masterful."
— *West Coast Review of Books* on *Trans-Siberian Express*

"A fast-paced suspense story… only a seasoned
newspaperman could have written with such inside
skills."
— *The Washington Star* on *The Henderson Equation*

"High-tension political intrigue with excellent
dramatization of the worlds of good and evil."
— *Calgary Herald* on *The Casanova Embrace*

"A man who willingly rips the veil from political
intrigue."
— *Bethesda Tribune* on *Undertow*

Warren Adler's political thrillers are...

"Ingenious."
—Publishers Weekly

"Diverting, well-written and sexy."
—Houston Chronicle

"Exciting."
—London Daily Telegraph

Praise for Warren Adler's Fiona Fitzgerald Mystery Series

"High-class suspense."
—*The New York Times* on *American Quartet*

"Adler's a dandy plot-weaver, a real tale-teller."
—*Los Angeles Times* on *American Sextet*

"Adler's depiction of Washington—its geography, social whirl, political intrigue—rings true."
—*Booklist* on *Senator Love*

"A wildly kaleidoscopic look at the scandals and political life of Washington D.C."
—*Los Angeles Times* on *Death of a Washington Madame*

"Both the public and the private story in Adler's second book about intrepid sergeant Fitzgerald make good reading, capturing the political scene and the passionate duplicity of those who would wield power."
—*Publishers Weekly* on *Immaculate Deception*

Also by Warren Adler

FICTION

THE FIONA FITZGERALD MYSTERY SERIES
American Quartet
American Sextet
Death of a Washington Madame
Immaculate Deception
Red Herring
Senator Love
The Ties that Bind
The Witch of Watergate
Washington Masquerade

SHORT STORY COLLECTIONS
Jackson Hole: Uneasy Eden
Never Too Late for Love
New York Echoes 1
New York Echoes 2
New York Echoes 3
The Sunset Gang
The Washington Dossier Diaries

PLAYS
Dead in the Water
Libido
The Sunset Gang: The Musical
The War of the Roses
Windmills

LAST CALL

BY WARREN ADLER

Inquiries: customerservice@warrenadler.com

STONEHOUSE PRODUCTIONS

Published Stonehouse Productions
www.warrenadler.com

-1-

It was the day he must have misplaced his sunglasses. He remembered that the blinding morning late September sun burned his eyes and that he had turned toward the West Side of Central Park where he first spotted Shaina, a white standard poodle. She was off her leash and running stiffly toward Ben, his black-coated 12-year-old of the same breed.

Birds of a feather, Harvey thought, chuckling at his strange metaphor. He didn't know she was Shaina then, nor did he know yet the lady who walked behind her holding a leash. He had not the slightest hint of the profound effect she would have on his life.

The early morning routine, now more of a slow walk, was a regular activity for Harvey Franklin and Ben. His alarm was always set for 5:30 a.m., although it was redundant. Ben's snout slobbered on Harvey's cheek at exactly that time every morning to get him up for their daily ritual.

"Okay, okay," Harvey would protest, although this daily reassurance of unconditional love was always a welcome wake-up call. In Harvey's narrowing world, Ben had become his boon, companion, best friend, and sounding board. Ben slept on a pillow on the floor beside Harvey's bed.

To a stranger who did not understand such dog-people relationships, the one-way conversation might have sounded bizarre or delusional. Of course, Harvey knew implicitly that Ben understood every word, every nuance, every change of mood.

Ben's replies were equally clear to Harvey, who knew every "word" of Ben's body language—the gaze, the tail wag, the movement of the paw, the posture, the occasional bark. As a young boy, Harvey had been fascinated by the wonderful dog books of Albert Payson Terhune, a name that few remember today. There was more to it than simply describing the relationship as man's best friend. There was a mysterious personal bond there between man and dog that defied clichés.

Ben was present during all of Harvey's morning ablutions, observing his movements as he put on his outdoor walking clothes, now embellished with a heavy wool sweater against the morning chill. Only then did his four-legged buddy drag him to the elevator, which would take them down six floors to the lobby of Number One Fifth and then across the street to the entrance to Central Park.

In the park, Harvey and Ben would amble along the path to Mineral Springs Lawn, the park's official designation as an East Side spot where unleashed dogs were allowed to play until 9 a.m. They paused often for Ben to make his frequent leg-lifting pit stops. At Ben's age, they had become more and more frequent. Once they arrived, Harvey would unleash Ben to mingle with the other canines, an activity that had begun in his puppyhood.

The routine had preceded Ben by two generations of his ancestors for more than 35 years, ever since Harvey and his wife had bought the condo at Number One Fifth and lived there through every permutation of Central Park's recent history of decline and renewal. He had survived the dark days of crime infestation in the last two decades of the 20th century when to brave the park in the dark was an act of courage, or perhaps insanity.

His late wife Anne, while enamored by each of their male standard poodles over the lifetime of their marriage, was somehow not as intimate with them as Harvey was. Perhaps it had something to do with male bonding, but Harvey had never thought much about it until Anne had passed on.

Harvey was not immune to the fears generated by media coverage of the various Central Park murders, rapes, and robberies that had occurred in what was once conceived as an exquisite oasis from the overwhelming cacophony of the raucous Big Apple. While reported crimes seemed to have dissipated somewhat lately, an occasional story called attention to the fact that the park, cleansed of the homeless, was still a tempting magnet for criminals.

He was all for beefing up a police presence in the park and elsewhere, and, as a committed conservative, he was a keen supporter of the stop-and-frisk policy which had been abandoned by a more liberal administration.

Even these days when a conservative movement of private citizens had come to the park's rescue, he felt a trill of insecurity when darkness descended. He was always alert to the changing seasons and the inevitable diminishment of light that came with the onset of fall and winter.

In his morning walks with Ben, he timed them so as to reach the grounds of the park's leash-free dog area at the moment when the rising sun began to peek over the high-rises that rimmed the park. At night, in the fall and winter months, he kept his outings with Ben on the park's periphery and was always grateful when Ben performed his business in short order.

When his wife was alive, they rarely employed dog walkers, except when business and social engagements demanded the service. On dogless vacations, they had sought out the most rigidly professional kennels. Now, as a widower who rarely left town, Harvey had relieved himself of that anxiety. He and Ben were now a perpetual twosome, sharing their declining years as two over-the-hill bachelors.

At 12 years of age, Ben had lost a great deal of his youthful spirit. He was slower, stiff-limbed from arthritis, and often winded, and although he had never been fixed, his sexual enthusiasm had waned as well. Twelve was pretty old for a poodle, and his black coat, now flecked with gray, had lost much of its earlier luster.

Harvey watched his geriatric dog move around the open lawn, always reminding him of their intertwined fate—two old farts walking into the far horizon like in a movie fade-out, waiting for the credits to roll. In dog time, Ben was 84. Harvey had just passed his 83rd birthday. His doctor claimed that considering his current health and his genes (his mother had died at 95), he was destined to equal that longevity if he didn't abuse himself.

The question of who would go first often reluctantly intruded as the central but inevitable dilemma on his mind as he stood with the other dog parents along the edge of the park lawn. If Harvey was the first to go, he had no illusions about Ben's fate. And if the dog went first? That would remain an open question, since finding a living creature with so much devotion might be impossible, and he could not even contemplate raising another puppy at his age.

Often, he berated himself for having such depressing thoughts. He did not delude himself that he was still in the ballgame. The fact was that he was benched and had been since Anne had died since she had been the social motivator of their marriage. She had been the arranger, and he had been the obedient follower. His social world, built around his colleagues at the ad agency, had faded away during his retirement years. Many of his retired colleagues had moved to warmer climes or died.

Still, he was determined to maintain a semblance of physical and mental vigor, mostly, he told himself, for Ben's sake. He did twice-a-week Pilates. He read the *Wall Street Journal* and the *New York Times* cover to cover. The latter's apparent left-wing bias, he acknowledged, gave him just the right prod to spark some healthy but, alas, diminishing rage. He tried valiantly to maintain some old-fashioned sense of the irate that might serve to anchor him in the vast ocean of an increasingly alien world. Lately, he found himself less moved by politics and the horrors of an outlandishly violent planet. As his time horizon shrunk, so did his concerns about the fate of civilization and its rapidly dehumanizing conflicts.

A Republican by generational tradition, he had learned to navigate in the New York world of liberals and ambitious strivers, many of them Jews, once barely a presence in the big-time ad agency business. The fact was that he was hardly aware of any restrictive policies when he entered the business.

A native of Kansas where his dad was a shoe salesman and his mother a homemaker, he was an only child, a good, industrious, well-brought-up, Midwestern, church-attending, play-by-the-rules boy. Like many ambitious young men of his time with a creative bent, he was drawn to the Big Apple and the once glamorous world of advertising touted in the popular media. Like many of his peers, he went east to New York and worked his way up in the ad business, making it to the upper tier with all the awards to prove it.

He was once told he looked like Kansas—blonde, freckled, tall, easily identified by accent and dress, and somewhat alien to the New York culture. In fact, he had been characterized, even by close friends in his early days in the Big Apple, as a hayseed.

Harvey first met Anne at what was called a mixer at an all-girls Lutheran college she was attending in Missouri. The school was across the river from the University of Kansas where Harvey was studying advertising and business. Anne was actually from the East Side of Manhattan—Yorktown—once largely populated by families who had immigrated from Germany years before. She was the daughter of a partner in a restaurant on 86th Street that served German cuisine.

Everything about their courtship was, as they say, according to Hoyle—traditional and predictable. They married at a church in Manhattan followed by a reception in the family restaurant. Anne had, as was the custom in those days, come to their marriage bed a virgin. To her, sex was an obligatory act of a faithful wife that she practiced more with consent than passion.

Harvey had risen quickly in the advertising business, and they were a popular couple in their circle of colleagues. Anne worked for the restaurant until it was sold a few years into their marriage. After that, Anne's concentration was offering social help to her husband's career, which she did with both efficiency and success.

For Anne's sake, in his heyday with the ad agency, Harvey had been persuaded to join the Knickerbocker Club, a stronghold of high society and anti-Semitic bias, as well as the New York Athletic Club, once equally restricted. He would not have characterized himself as anti-Semitic or anti-Black or anti any ethnic group. It was the way things were, and he and Anne lived within that mindset and the traditions of the times. He merely went with the flow, feeling no animosity toward any group. Above all, he avoided any confrontations as he navigated in his ever more diverse world.

Anne, on the other hand, was not only aware of the way things were, but privately she was strongly biased. She would always treat Harvey's growing coterie of Jewish colleagues with politeness and respect, although she would privately complain that the ad game, once an enclave that restricted Jews, was, as she put it, "being inundated by kikes." Of course, none of Harvey's Jewish colleagues were ever invited to the Knick or the New York Athletic Club. Everyone knew the score on that issue.

In their world at the time, there was somewhat of an acceptable divide between what was business-social and what was social-social. In the former, Jews were, as they gained a presence in the ad industry, an integral part of the landscape. In their social circles, they were, except on very rare occasions, excluded. While Harvey was well aware of the dividing line, he did not dwell on the subject as an advocate either way.

Nor did he allow Anne's biased view about Jews to influence his relationships with his Jewish colleagues whom he respected and often applauded. His strategy to keep the peace in his marriage was to ignore her periodic defamatory comments, caution her to keep such remarks private, and mildly contest her assertions.

As times changed, Anne did become less vocal and more discreet on the subject, especially in public, and grew to grudgingly accept the changing conditions as a further indication of a decline in American cultural values. Of course, in Harvey's business, understanding the metrics of such acceptance was a key component of advertising strategy. Every minority in the American rainbow had become a legitimate sales target.

With Anne, his strategy was to never rock the boat, and he avoided anything that raised her ire. Not that he was the cliché of a milquetoast, but he wanted no controversy at home to interfere with his dedication to his advertising creativity. He prided himself on his ability to focus.

Harvey resigned from the Knick shortly after Anne died. He no longer had any use for it socially. A few years later, he resigned from the New York Athletic Club, which no longer seemed to fit his age or lifestyle.

By then, he had joined the Century Association, an old-line club for those who could bridge the very strict entrance requirements. Many of his fellow members were ex-advertising guys with whom he had much in common.

These days he lunched at Century, mostly for conversation, and while his circle of friends from his agency days had severely diminished, he had retained at least one regular, George Hapsworth, who was a decade older than Harvey and a former account man at Y and R where he had spent most of his career. George's principal asset was a curmudgeon's eloquent rage, a penchant for dire predictions, and a nasty opinion of the human race. At times, Harvey suspected he was drawn to George because George put into words what Harvey might have occasionally thought.

George truly believed that America was hurtling toward financial and intellectual collapse and anarchy and that all politicians were idiots and every aspect of American life was being manipulated by thieves and charlatans. His personal solution was to spend all his considerable wealth, acquired by market tips from big business insider clients, before the government took it and, hopefully, leave his heirs a massive unfunded debt. This latter aspiration, as he had averred repeatedly, would constitute the victorious life.

After Anne's death, Harvey had been an occasional invitee as a single man to dinner parties, but even those invitations had dried up. At that stage in his life the companionship of women was not a priority.

Occasionally, he did wake up with a hard-on, and he was thankful for Internet porn for an intermittent sexual solo. He had eschewed women for that purpose. He had been rushed in the early days of his widowhood, and while he experienced some success, a number of disastrous attempts had convinced him that it was better to avoid the challenge and stick to occasional solos.

All in all, he could fill up his days with enough mental activity to keep his mind and body in shape. His father had died in his 60s, but Harvey was relying on his mother's longevity to govern his life clock, and to that end, he kept a strict regimen to maintain his health. His father had overused John Barleycorn and coffin sticks.

Despite the severe narrowing of his social life to almost

nonexistent, he did not categorize himself as lonely, deprived, or depressed. And, of course, he had Ben, upon whom he lavished most of his attention, which was returned in spades.

The various parents who stood by as their dogs cavorted with each other in Central Park were familiar to Harvey, and he had, from time to time, struck up casual social friendships with them, but no real bonding.

He no longer traveled to visit his only son, Richard, and his youngest grandchildren in London who seemed little interested in the fate of their grandfather. The visits were now curtailed for a variety of reasons, among them his son's constant nose-to-nose nagging for Harvey to sell his two-bedroom condo with the view of the park, now heading to a six-million-dollar price tag, a piece of which his son coveted to repair his own fragile financial situation and the consequences of his divorce.

The alimony Richard had to pay his ex-wife had devastated his exchequer, further complicated by the staggering tuition for his three children from his current marriage to attend posh private schools in the United Kingdom. He also had two children by his first marriage who were living in the States but rarely called their grandfather. In fact, they no longer called at all, a situation he had learned to live with by avoiding thinking about them.

Harvey calculated that he and Anne had already done their fair share of helping financially to keep Richard and his show-off lifestyle afloat. What galled Harvey the most was the way Richard posed the request to sell his apartment.

"It's the top of the market in Manhattan now, Dad. You don't need the space. You can cash in at the peak and easily find a one-bedroom rental to carry you over without tightening your belt. You still have your investments, your pension, Social Security, and Medicare. I mean, let's face it, I'll be getting it anyway, and I'm not asking for more than half right now."

"Carry me over?"

"You know what I mean."

"Got an estimate, Richard? You were always good at math. And don't forget Uncle Sam who is also scheduled to get his piece."

"He's figured in," Richard replied. Obviously, he had calculated his take carefully, but his needs were immediate. "You told me your doctor gave you a decade at your last physical."

"He's motivated. I promised him a million if he gets me to 100. I think he believes it."

Richard had ignored that comment but then countered with his own.

"There are tax advantages to early giving."

Richard had made this the heart of his argument ad infinitum. Such discussions, now growing more frequent on the phone, had become whiny and often desperate and did manage in weak moments to get a check out of Harvey. He was, after all, a father of the old school, clinging to the role of the filial protector, another Midwestern attribute. Anne had been tougher. But then she was of German ancestry.

The fact was that Richard did make a decent living as an engineer for BP, but the financial devastations of his personal life had taken their toll. In some ways, they had wreaked havoc on Harvey's sense of filial devotion, a characteristic that had come down through the generations. But then it was a different time in a more ordered world that had long passed. With discipline and, thankfully, distance, Harvey managed to avoid much of his son's overwrought life.

He did try early on to keep up the façade of devoted fatherhood by annual visits to London, but he began to feel more and more that he was intruding on a dysfunctional family with whom he had little in common, and he ceased his visits. Lately, it had become apparent that the only living creature that truly cared about him and needed his presence was the devoted four-legged Ben, and besides, he hated to leave Ben in a strange kennel for any length of time.

At that moment in his life, as he ambled along in Central Park on this chilly September morning, he felt a kind of philosophic calm. He had made peace with himself, had adjusted to his situation as an old widower with a four-legged buddy, a lifestyle of singleness and reasonable contentment, and an inclination to persevere in the moment, avoiding untoward thoughts of the shrinking future.

As he stood on the sidelines watching Ben interact with other dogs, he noted a white standard poodle, also a bit stiff-legged, move closer to Ben and begin the usual get-to-know-you sniffing routine. It was when Ben made an effort to mount the white poodle that the parent, a woman roughly Harvey's age, moved to slap Ben's rump.

"She's fixed, you schmuck," the woman chided, directing her satirical ire directly to Ben, snickering, looking upward, offering a half smile to Harvey. He noted that the woman had good white teeth, probably implants. She wore large sunglasses. Gray curly hair peeked out of a red baseball cap with a Yankee baseball logo. Like him, she wore a sweater, a grey cardigan, and a long plaid scarf that fell over an ample bust. She flashed a smile toward Harvey, as if to assure him that there were no hard feelings. Her gaze lingered, and Harvey felt as if he were being assessed, a strange and curious sensation.

"I usually bring Shaina to the Cedar Hill run on the West Side," she said, moving closer to Harvey. "Getting too crowded." She surveyed the scene, keeping an eye on her dog, who had given Ben a short shrift and was now sniffing around others. "She's a real flirt for an old bag."

For some reason not yet apparent to him, Harvey took the

unusual step of entering a dialogue. It was not his way—not shyness, but reticence.

"It's more nostalgia these days," Harvey began. "He used to be a lot more randy."

"Poor guy," the woman said.

"How old is she?" Harvey asked, raising his chin in the white poodle's direction.

"Keeping one's age secret is a woman's prerogative," the woman winked. Her accent was distinctly New York native.

"Ben's pushing 13," Harvey said.

"A bar mitzvah boy," she snickered. "Shaina's pushing 12," she admitted with a shrug. "She's my third."

"All bitches?"

"What else?" the woman smirked. "Takes one to know one."

Harvey chuckled.

"When she goes, that's *finit*."

"I know what you mean," Harvey said, as if her statement needed a retort.

"Do you?"

She hesitated and studied him.

"Completely," he nodded with a smile.

Harvey debated whether to tell her his age but demurred. When he told people his number, they usually marveled at his condition.

She took out a tissue and wiped her nose.

There was, of course, a bit of bravado in his age revelation. He was still ramrod straight with a full head of hair, which had turned distinguished white. He had managed to keep his belly reasonably flat with his twice-weekly Pilates class and his daily home floor exercises. He could pass for 10 or even 15 years younger if the light was right. He loved hearing that he didn't look his age. Had he expected this woman to react that way? She commented on the weather.

"Goddamned chilly."

"It's officially autumn," he said.

"Weathermen know bupkis."

He caught the unmistakable note of attitude, the proud mark of a native New Yorker. By then he had long shed his Midwestern naivety. More than five decades of an advertising career, mostly in the Big Apple, had schooled him in the nuances, habits, and peculiarities of the city's native inhabitants, and he had learned a smattering of unavoidable yiddishisms. The woman gave him a skeptical look, chuckled, and shook her head as she watched the dogs rushing about, exulting in their freedom.

"Shaina," she cried suddenly and insistently. The white poodle stopped in her tracks and glanced toward her. She made a come-hither gesture, and Shaina obeyed. The woman bent down, kissed her snout, and addressed her with a warning finger. "Stay away from the horny riffraff. Act your age."

Then she rose and turned to Harvey. "What's yours named?"

"Ben."

"Go play with Ben," she motioned, as if it were an insult to Ben's aging manhood. Obviously, Shaina knew the gesture but not the instructions, and she went off to sniff a laconic black cocker spaniel. "Wrong choice for Shaina. Those cockers don't know their ass from first base."

"Shaina," Harvey said. "That's an unusual name."

The woman turned toward him and snickered. "Not in my neck of the woods. It means *pretty* in Yiddish."

The woman took off her sunglasses and inspected Harvey's face. He saw that she had cerulean blue eyes that sparkled in the sunlight. His observation surprised him, and he felt the pull of an uncommon interest.

"You wouldn't have known," she said, inspecting him carefully, smiling broadly again.

"Not in my neck of the woods," he acknowledged, although the word was vaguely familiar. She scanned his face.

"I did catch the earlier one," he said. "You said weathermen didn't know bupkis."

"Did I?" she giggled. "You know what it means?"

"You'd be surprised," he said, pleased by the banter.

She smiled, searched his face, then nodded.

"Emerald Isle," she proclaimed. "It shouts from your punim."

"Punim?"

"Face," she chuckled.

"On my grandmother's side, the orange hue," he said. "I'm Harvey Franklin."

He lifted his right hand and reached out to her. She reciprocated, squeezing his hand firmly.

"Sarah Silverman."

While clasping her hand, he caught himself inspecting her more closely, which surprised him. Her eyes, those clear blue nuggets. He noted her tiny lines of crow's feet and a loosening around her lips. He figured her age at somewhere in the 70s, give or take. But something about her suggested youthfulness.

Suddenly, she leaned her head back and laughed. Her gesture surprised him.

"I get it. Ben Franklin."

"Better him than me," Harvey said, nodding toward Ben.

She shrugged and became silent as she watched the dogs at play. Time passed. They were silent. Then she checked her watch, which she wore with the face on the inside of her wrist. In a reflective action, Harvey checked the time on his cell phone.

"Ten more minutes till we're illegal. The park's unleashed rule ends at nine."

She was silent again, surveying the scene. The parents

were gathering their canines and hooking them up to their leashes.

"I'll say this," she said. "The East Side has a better class of dogs."

"I take that as a compliment," he said.

"I said dogs," she said with a wink. "Not people."

She offered him a parting smile and a wave as she leashed up Shaina and headed west. Harvey watched their receding figures for a long time, sensing some feeling of occurrence. It was as if a door had opened into a musty unoccupied room.

He had caught her very unsubtle geographical implication as if it had been aimed directly at him. He was well aware that the West Side was often thought of by some as ground zero for the liberal persuasion, traditionally peopled by Jewish lefties, obviously her side. It was one of those demarcations that stuck and become a cliché.

The other side, meaning the East Side, was, from the point of view of those on her side, the wrong side, a geographical enclave lined wall-to-wall with tight-assed, right-wing, biased, racist conservatives. He chuckled to himself, knowing that that inaccurate designation had obvious anti-Semitic connotations as well.

Anne, his loving wife of 50 years, had often used the derisive expression "West Side liberal kikes"—always in private, of course. She was a devoted churchgoing Lutheran. Harvey knew she was, deep down, an anti-Semite, and all attempts early in their marriage to disabuse her of the bias were futile. Thankfully, her attitude wasn't publicly obvious, but it was there, sub rosa, lurking just beneath the surface.

She had been born and reared in Yorkville, the East 86th Street area, the beating heart of the New York City German community. Harvey had learned from Anne's parents that many of their neighbors had supported Hitler and the Nazis before World War II, but they had vehemently denied it. Anne was quick to point out that both her parents were dogged air-raid wardens during the war.

Harvey was respectful and affectionate toward his wife and gentle with his criticisms of her various biases. And Anne managed somehow to keep herself publicly reined in. When he offered his usual mild protest to her occasional private ethnic insults, she would dismiss him as a bleeding heart softie, always in good humor, of course.

As for the Blacks and Latinos who lived in Harlem just a handful of blocks away, they were simply dismissed by her as irrelevant and better ignored as if they did not exist, except as cleaning ladies and delivery boys. Still, in every other aspect of their long marriage, she had been supportive, loving, and, he felt certain (considering her obvious disinterest), faithful.

He did not consider himself biased, judging people more by intelligence, skill, and personality. In his mental lexicon, Jews were smart, talented, ambitious, sometimes arrogant, and often a bit too aggressive, but he had many Jewish colleagues, co-workers, and friends over the years, and he was well aware that Jews hated when any Gentile bragged about that.

Nevertheless, he had grown up with these ingrained stereotypes that were often difficult to dislodge. But above all, he did not consider himself an anti-Semite or, for that matter, anti-race or ethnicity. He considered himself a salt-of-the-earth Midwesterner, a Kansan, traditionally considerate of others like Nellie Forbush in *South Pacific*. People said he looked like a male version of her.

Sarah Silverman had it partially right as far as he was concerned. He was definitely not on the West Side of things as he imagined the woman to be. He was, body and soul, the East Sider of her clichéd persuasion. Very much so. He was, perish the thought, a Republican, a conservative in its truest sense, but not a militant activist party-line Republican conservative. Before he had come to New York to make his fortune, everybody around him was a Republican. It was a way of life, and he was part of it.

He had grown up reading the Horatio Alger stories of self-reliance, hard work, ambition, and living life by practicing the golden rule. It offended him to see or hear anyone mock America, and he still teared up when the flag passed by in a parade. Even at his age and after all he had experienced, he still believed in the old verities that some in today's environment considered corny and old fashioned.

Some, he knew, might describe his personal brand of conservatism as a form of stasis, or keeping as much of the perceived good stuff the way it was. He knew such an idea was utterly impossible, but he clung to it anyway like a cat stuck in a tree. In fact, he would have been happy if nothing had changed after the 1950s.

He could have done without all the technology, all the medical advances, all the social changes. Okay, lady, he told himself, you can keep your save-the-world crap. The irony is that the woman had said nothing that might have set off such a personal inner conflagration. He had imposed something on her persona that had expanded beyond his ability to control it.

As for Anne and her prejudices, he had never given her cause to doubt his 100 percent devotion to their marriage, although he had come close.

He had not been immune to seduction and still retained in his dotage the imagination that enhanced fantasy. He was like poor Ben now, with sex on his mind but no longer able to offer a sure-thing performance. Odd, he noted, how his thoughts had drifted from conservatism to sex. Perhaps it was what he imagined was under her sweater.

Such flights of fancy were not new to him. He had been a creative director at Young & Rubicam and at other agencies as he came up the ad agency ladder. His currency was ideas, and he had always suspected that his brain was pitted with endless ridges of imagination. Sometimes he suspected that if he ever seriously shared his ideas and aspirations, he might be a candidate for commitment to a mental facility.

He spent most of his life projecting what others thought and felt, rearranging the obvious, creating scenarios, finding inventive ways to express the clichés of life. That was his talent. His commercial mission in the ad game was mass persuasion, and he had been damned good at it according to his peers and as the awards on his apartment walls attested. There was not enough space for all of them. In fact some of his plaques and faded framed certificates of special achievement were piled in his closets.

Of course, that was very much yesterday, and the wall displays were mostly Anne's doing. She was militant about his success. He had become, in his own parlance, a *usta*—a person who used to be *someone*. Now he had entered the realm of the unremembered.

In the 14 odd years of his retirement, the energy that had powered his career seemed to have faded from lack of use. Now, suddenly, whamo! The long-closed door had blasted open.

The fact was that this lady, this Jewess parent of the white poodle, had rattled his cage in a very mysterious way. Was it the Jew thing? What he did know was that his two-bedroom condo at One Fifth Avenue was exactly across the street from Temple Emanu-El, next to which a police trailer was permanently parked just in case some terrorist bastard got it into his head to bomb the place.

Except for that running sense of fear, the other issues the woman had stirred up in his mind seemed oddly relevant, a significant occurrence. He felt disturbingly engaged, and he didn't know why.

Both he and Ben had a restless night. It was no secret that age brought with it urges in the night, and he often found himself awakened once or twice to go pee. His most persistent fear was that Ben would awake with the same affliction and force him to make an outdoor pit stop on the fringes of Central Park.

He took the precaution of an end-of-the-day quick walk in the hope that Ben's bladder would hold until morning. Sometimes he had actually joined Ben in a mutual piss.

Ben's urges were becoming more and more frequent, and sure enough, on the night of the day he met the woman with the white poodle, he had to get up, throw a sweater over his pajamas, and take Ben out into the scary night. In fact, it actually happened twice that night. Was Ben telling him something?

The next morning, to his absolute surprise and delight, he awoke with an erection. It lingered for awhile and signaled that he was still somewhat alive, always a comforting sign. Still some lead in the old pencil, he sighed with a chuckle.

For some reason, the evidence of his sexual viability energized him, and he was out of bed and ready before Ben had shaken himself awake. The dog seemed confused by this change of tactic and, once outside in the park, had to endure an uncommon tug of impatience on his leash as he sniffed along the path, his nose scoping his pee territory.

The sun had barely risen over the eastern high-rises when they arrived at the designated lawn. Only two dogs had arrived, and Ben looked confused and somewhat lonely since he was largely ignored by the early arrivals. Harvey kept his sights on the western path, squinting for any sign of the white poodle and her parent.

It was colder than the day before, and the chill seemed to prod his anxiety as he looked impatiently at the time on his cell phone. Worse, he felt an illogical surge of anger assail him, as if the woman had deliberately stood him up. Then he berated himself for his foolishness, his anxiety, and his impatience. Finally, he decided to cease looking toward the west, concentrating instead on the antics of the dogs.

Then a white dog crossed his field of vision, and he heard her voice.

"Actually, I hadn't planned to come this way this morning. It's a bit of a trek. But Shaina has a mind of her own."

The white dog had headed directly to Ben, making no bones about her preference.

"Typical. Yesterday she played hard to get," the woman said, smiling broadly.

"I guess she knows class when she sees it."

"You remembered," the woman chuckled, turning toward him. Her dark glasses hid her eyes.

"I didn't take it personally," Harvey said.

"It wasn't meant to be," Sarah said. "Besides, it was stupid. I insulted the entire East Side of Manhattan."

"I got it."

"Did you?" Sarah asked.

The sun had finally risen above the eastern high-rises, lighting up her face, sparkling her smile. They stood silently for awhile, watching their dogs. He searched his mind for words to keep her engaged. Surprisingly, she was the first to break the silence. He felt foolish, since the rules of engagement were obvious.

"You live near here?"

"Number One Fifth." He paused. "You?"

"The Century. That art deco building on 63rd and Central Park West."

"A long walk," he commented, deliberately cautious. In the persona he had assigned her, she would be quick to take offense, and he submitted to caution since he did not want to lose the connection. What surprised him was her curiosity about him. He noted that she wore the same sweater.

"What do you do?" she asked flatly, casually.

"Retired. I was in the advertising business."

"A mad man."

"Actually, we didn't call it that. A contemporary invention."

"I saw it. Did they get it right?"

"Yes and no. The office booze was wrong. I was in the creative end. We needed clear heads. The sales account men were the three-martini lunch guys."

"And the sex?"

For some reason, the question seemed to signal the action of taking off her sunglasses and revealing those blue eye nuggets that had arrested his attention yesterday morning.

"Over the top," he said. Not really, he knew, fearing that he was being set up for a sharp feminist reaction. He got it anyway.

"I grew up in that era, and I think they got that one right."

"You were in advertising?"

"Lawyer."

His heart sank. His mind filled with a long list of injustices, civil rights, discrimination, police brutality, anti-war, equal pay, race, feminism, poverty, immigration, the whole caboodle of complaints.

"Divorce," she said, her lips pursed, as if she had read his mind. "I was known in the business as the nut cutter."

"I'm glad my wife never needed your services."

"Long marriage?"

"More than five decades."

"Pure bliss, I suppose."

"More or less," he shrugged. He had always been conflicted on how to answer that frequently asked question, especially by unattached women. The once happily married were apparently a more enticing target. She grew pensive.

"I was up to bat three times. Struck out twice. My third was a keeper."

"Still keeping?" he said, disappointed.

He watched her turn her eyes away and swallow hard. He noted the tension. She was silent for a brief moment and then offered a follow-up comment.

"Gone." She met his gaze for a long moment. Her smile seemed tentative. "Lots in common. Especially how we viewed the world."

"And how was that?"

He sensed his own change of tone.

"Do I have to spell it out?" She giggled, and their eyes locked.

"Not really. You read it on my—punin, was it?"

"Poo-nim," she said, correcting his pronunciation.

"However," he said. "I'm always open to another point of view."

"And you believe that?"

"Don't you?"

He searched her face for any sign of hostility and couldn't find any. She laughed.

"I told you I was a divorce lawyer. I was bombarded with other points of view."

"I can imagine."

"Can you?" she laughed. "Actually, I was a referee, and I never stopped the fight until there was blood all over the mat and they were both out of breath and badly wounded. Only then were they able to make a deal."

"Okay then," Harvey said, raising both hands, palms out. "I surrender in advance. I'm everything your instinct tells you. Not a Neanderthal. Open minded. Eager to be persuaded."

"Bullshit," she said, looking toward the canine crowd. "Can't teach an old dog new tricks."

"Try me," Harvey said. He was enjoying the repartee.

"You're flirting." She moved her head back and laughed into the sky.

"I'm trying, but believe me, I'm way out of practice."

"You're not alone," she said, nodding.

They grew silent for a long time, watching the dogs. The sudden silence seemed strange, and the fact was that they had indeed been flirting, eagerly, perhaps like when they were teenagers before being burdened with the baggage of living. For obvious reasons, he needed to expand on his current status.

"It's been nearly seven years."

She appeared to assess him with deeper purpose. Of course, he had pretty well given away his age. He imagined her in her middle 70s.

"You seem none the worse for wear," she said.

"Ben keeps me moving."

She nodded, looking toward Shaina who was stiffly gamboling with Ben.

"Looks like she found a buddy," Sarah mumbled. He noted a subtle shift of subject.

"Why not? Not over till it's over."

She turned to look at him and shot him an oddly judgmental look.

"You are a cornucopia of clichés, kiddo."

"It has been said that's where the truth lies."

"The comeback kid," she muttered, looking at her watch. He was thinking comeback in another sense, enjoying the word play. Their back and forth had a certain intimacy. He pulled out his cell phone and looked at it.

"Still have a half hour," he said.

"I think Shaina is ready," Sarah said. She turned toward him and offered her hand. "Nice talking to you." He took her hand firmly but sensed that she was reluctant.

"Very much," he said. Their gaze met, but she turned quickly and signaled to Shaina. The dog obeyed, and she kneeled to hook her leash. Then, without looking back, she headed west.

-2-

Frank Silverman, grey-faced, pale, and wan, sat slumped in the wing chair in front of the television watching a black-and-white film on the Turner Classic Movies channel. Sarah recognized Myrna Loy and William Powell on the screen, which was never dark except when Frank slept.

Frank was currently in the grip of multiple ailments—heart failure, late onset diabetes, and gout, and his once agile and retentive mind and memory were now moving relentlessly into the black hole of dementia.

"Honey, I'm home," Sarah trilled as she entered the living room. The satirical cliché signaled Frank that she was back in their apartment, which seemed to soothe him and brought a welcoming smile to his lips.

He was clearly anxious when she was away and calmed by her return. It was part of the necessary routine that seemed essential for his peace of mind. He looked at her, nodded, blinked, broadened his smile, and took her hand, squeezing it lightly and bringing it to his lips to kiss it. She pecked him on the forehead. He released her hand, raised his eyes, and looked at the television screen again.

"Enjoying the movie, Frank?"

He did not answer. He was losing his ability to speak complicated sentences.

She knew he had seen that movie multiple times. She knew, too, that each time he saw it, it was completely new to him. At times, when she would join him, holding his hand, he would forget who the characters were halfway through the film, and she would patiently identify them.

"Where were you, Sarah?" It was another of his repetitive questions.

"Walking Shaina."

She was used to it and no longer berated him for his forgetfulness. Such was the expected progression, and she had grown to accept it and ignore it.

At the sound of her name, Shaina moved toward Frank, and he automatically patted her head and continued to look at the television screen. In fact, watching old movies seemed the only thing that captured his attention these days, although Sarah didn't have a clue about what was registering in his mind and fought mightily against her own impatience and the natural frustration and depression of being a witness to his obvious decline.

Helena, his caretaker at the time, had encouraged Sarah to keep reminding him of their early days together in an effort to stimulate his recall and get him to respond. Sarah had even enhanced the process by prodding him to discuss his scholarly specialty, the American Civil War. He had been a professor of American history at NYU. Sometimes, her efforts opened up his memory door to a smidgen of recall, but those reactions were getting more and more rare.

At 83, Frank's moments of mental clarity were diminishing swiftly, no matter how much Sarah welcomed and exploited them. She had been forewarned by his doctors that such moments were fleeting and the day would come when the curtain would finally fall on his once brilliant mind.

Sarah had divided her life into before-Frank and after-Frank. In her before-Frank life, she had lived what, in retrospect, might be called her protest period, committed to tearing down the ramparts of all her perceived restrictions on freedom, injustice, and bias.

Like many of her peers in the '60s, she had lived in a fever of political and personal rebellion—anti-war, anti-establishment, anti-the-so-called-power-structure, anti-middle-class, and every other anti one could think of. She lived in a riotous eddy of drug-fueled sexual promiscuity and perpetual, exhilarating protest.

The Vietnam War was the central theme. *Against* was the operative umbrella. America was the brutal tyrant, the indiscriminate killer of the innocent. Ironically, pacifist had become militant.

It was over-the-top glorious, beyond mere excess, one long high, and, in the end, paying the debt to the piper on the road to self-destruction. Frank had caught her in his net of reason just in time, guided her out of excess and the dangers of addiction, and proved to her that love, patience, and discipline could help tame the wild horse within her and keep her active in the battle for what she conceived as moral perfection.

By any standard, as she looked back on those days, she was blessed with both an excess of brains and beauty, and her most coveted assets were her figure, her high full breasts, her small waist, her long tapered legs, and her astonishing blue eyes about which she had offered numerous imaginative anecdotes of their provenance, the most prominent of which was a long-ago deflowering of a pious Jewish maiden by a blue-eyed Russian lover reminiscent of the affair of Tevye's daughter in *Fiddler on the Roof.*

Those days had been a form of ecstasy, a wild rapture, and she had come down from that high in a state of profound delirium, disoriented, disillusioned, and depressed, lost in the inevitable reality of youth's demise and the looming future of adult resignation. When she finally met Frank, who became her savior, his loving patience and wise counsel repaired and restored her. She owed him.

Still intact, however, was her strong aversion for injustice, bias, and intolerance. It continued to inspire her thinking. It was still fueled by militant advocacy, but maturity had put a more measured spin on righting such perceived wrongs, and her causes were no longer nourished by drugs and the unbridled passions of youth. The mortal enemy of her liberalism, however, was still out there as a force to be reckoned with, and although the tools of opposition had become more pragmatic, her political energy had not faltered.

Both she and Frank were not religious, but they classified themselves as committed secular Jews and strong supporters of Israel, even though as left wingers they were very conflicted and against Israel's settlement policy. Despite eschewing ritual, they had always been ardent supporters of Israel's survival, willing to protect what they knew in their guts was the last refuge from the perpetual onslaught of anti-Semitism. Both had grown up in orthodox homes where Yiddish was spoken.

As anti-Semitism reared its ugly head and spread throughout Europe and the Middle East and elsewhere, fueled by a jihad psychology that had borrowed the hateful excesses of the Nazis and taken them one step further by threatening to obliterate the last refuge of the Jews—Israel—Sarah found herself becoming more and more outspoken and defensively tribal.

Meeting Frank, a gentle, wise, scholarly man, was to her the gift of stability and what she had determined to be safe love. Frank built her a secure nest in which to repair herself and prosper, and she vowed that she would live up to the standards he had celebrated. His views were pretty much like hers but far more measured and nuanced and a lot less confrontational. They had been married for 52 years and raised two daughters. She had gone to law school and built a comfortable solo practice, now defunct.

Frank's scholarly obsession with the Civil War had motivated many excursions to those long-ago battlefields about which he had become an expert in the various military strategies employed by each side. Recounting the slaughter had stiffened his contemporary anti-war resolve and made his views controversial among his peers and colleagues, which had contributed to his career failures but strengthened the bond between him and Sarah.

By any metric, it was a good run for both of them. They had traveled frequently and enjoyed many of the same things. Although Frank had encountered some physical ailments along the way, Sarah had determined that they had beaten the odds and would enjoy a reasonably active old age together.

Of course, they could not escape the reality of the aging body. Just turned 80, she was remarkably healthy. Her doctor predicted that with luck she would live well into her 90s.

Frank had shown some early signs of dementia, but they both dismissed them as merely the intermittent ravages of the aging mind. For a long time, Sarah was in denial, but it soon became too obvious to ignore. Frank became more forgetful, and there was no escaping the coming onslaught of Alzheimer's. Doctors had privately confirmed the diagnosis to her. Frank was losing his insight, and she suspected that he was well aware of his plight.

For Sarah, accepting the reality of his decline was heartbreaking. It was as if they had suddenly found themselves on different trains. Frank had caught the express, and she was traveling on the local; Frank's train was speeding on the track to nowhere, and her train was moving smoothly on its regular route.

She characterized the aging process and the end game of death as God's joke. For Sarah and millions like her, there was no other way to assess the situation without telling yourself lies. She was never good at that. Her only option was to face the inevitability of Frank's entry into the dark tunnel of dementia.

Sarah had made a solemn vow to herself that under no

circumstances would she hand Frank over to strangers in a nursing facility, and she would keep him at home until the end. So far, despite the challenges, she had kept that commitment, a sacrifice that she assured herself was necessary for her own sense of loyalty and devotion. For her, any other course would be desertion and would haunt her for the rest of her life.

Helena, his now indispensable Haitian caretaker, had become the guardian and enforcer of this acknowledged commitment and had taken it on as her mission. Sarah had explained very precisely that she had sworn to herself and her children that she would never ever put Frank in the hands of strangers. It took considerable research to find Helena, and Sarah considered herself lucky to have her.

At first, Sarah was somewhat put off by Helena's references to God, which was ironic since Sarah had been referring to Frank's dementia as God's joke to rationalize her thoughts about impending death, which, although somewhat satirical, seemed a natural explanation for the cycle of birth, growth, maturity, disintegration, and total collapse.

At their initial interview, Sarah restrained herself from the analogy. When Sarah checked her references, Helena's former employers had emphasized her religious obsession. She had been a nun in Haiti, and although she was no longer in an order, she was committed, as she put it, "to do God's work on earth." All of her references cited her God vision as the key to her compassion, and she quickly revealed to Sarah that her mission was commanded by God to ease the road to oblivion. As one of her former employers opined, "Better a caretaker who believes she is doing God's work than one who is just in it for the money. When you differ or disobey her rules for your patient, she will sincerely believe you are interfering with God's command. The other side of the coin is that she is expensive but gives away most of her salary to Haitian charities."

"You must understand, Madame," Helena had explained in her precise, vaguely accented English. "This process will require a willingness on your part to make considerable sacrifices, especially on your time and your freedom. This is God's will. We cannot arrest the mental disintegration of this disease, and eventually it will take his mind completely. I have considerable experience in this, Madame. It is terminal, and it is an undertaking you should take with the full knowledge of what will happen. God willing, he should enter the other world without pain."

"I have made up my mind," Sarah reiterated with conviction. "I will keep him with me until the end."

Helena nodded and was silent for a moment before proceeding.

"Believe me, Madame, I have been through this before. It is my profession and I have developed a kind of expertise in this. If I take this on, I will need your full cooperation. With hard work, we will be able to cope with his loss of cognition, but I will demand your cooperation. I have had cases where the spouse cannot cope with what is inevitable. My orders come from a higher source, and I follow these orders to the letter."

"I understand, Helena," Sarah said, attracted by the woman's sense of mission, however it was motivated. Not a great fan of religious zeal, Sarah was convinced that in regard to Frank's care, she would rather opt for such dedication. Above all, what she feared most was to expose her husband to indifference.

"I owe this man my life, Helena. I will do everything you suggest if it extends his…." She hesitated.

"Comfort and well being," Helena said, nodding. "As his mind closes and his awareness and body functions decline, your dedication will be tested."

"I am fully prepared for what's to come," Sarah said in nearly a whisper.

"Believe me, I know how you feel. God will instruct us." Helena was sitting stiffly in the chair during her initial interview, breathing deeply before speaking. "I worked for years in nursing homes specializing in dementia. Call it Alzheimer's if you will, but the disintegration is the same. They are..." Her voice dropped, and her nostrils expanded. "...death factories where evil abounds. Patients suffer starvation, dehydration, drugs to hasten their departure. The patients themselves, before they have totally lost it, might have decreed or signed documents to withhold any means that would prolong life if their minds disappear completely. Then there are the loved ones who, for whatever reason, some reluctantly, some deliberately, wishing to relieve the burden for themselves or their loved ones, collaborate to hasten their death."

She paused, took a deep breath, and continued. "I can no longer, Mrs. Silverman, abide by such decisions to hasten death. It is against the wishes of the Almighty and those who do this will rot in hell forever. Only God can take life. Only God. I vowed I would only work for those who understand this. If you are not committed to that idea, I cannot take this job. But if you are, I promise I will help make your husband's demise as comfortable as possible. I am willing to follow this case the way God and nature intended. That is my commitment. Yours must be to attend to him in his home environment until the end. I have done this before with others. I assume you have checked my former clients."

Of course, Sarah had done so. Three of Helena's former employers had kept her to the end. Another, a male spouse, had finally surrendered and dispatched his wife to a facility, much to Helena's regret and over her protestations.

"Without Helena," one of the references, a female, told her, "I would never have survived. It is devastating," the woman explained. "Helena will save your life."

"*My* life?" Sarah had remonstrated.

"Yes, *your* life," the woman reiterated. "Sorry to say this, but your husband's life is over. Don't you understand, Mrs. Silverman? When the mind goes, that's it. Kaput. There is no person there anymore. You have lost him."

"This is not what I want to hear," Sarah said, prompted by some latent belligerence.

"I know. But you asked about Helena. She pulled me through. Hire her. Her expertise is in great demand, believe me. I must warn you that she has some crackpot spiritual theories about God and reincarnation. Pay no attention. And, oh yes, it is an expensive proposition, and I hope you have the resources. Thank God I was able to do this for Harry. We had a large house in Westchester and had to literally create a hospital environment in one part of it. I followed her directions to the letter. I owed it to my husband."

Another reference, a man, was even more forthcoming. "I could not have survived this without her. She is a professional and has found a remarkable business niche. In the two years she was with me caring for Mildred, I paid her more than $300,000 in the three years she was with us, and she was worth every cent. I would have paid more if I had to. She recycles the money to charities. She believes she is doing God's work. Most people don't understand it from that point of view. Mildred, my wife, was the love of my life, and I had vowed never ever to desert her. Never. Helena made me understand what I needed to do to extend her..." A sob rose up in his throat for a moment before he continued. "...She was right in every respect. Believe me. I got what I paid for. Don't take her on unless you are willing to subject yourself to her rules for you and your spouse. Be aware, she is one tough cookie. Her employer is God, and she believes it implicitly. Obey her to the letter, and she will help you through."

"I've been told she has some strange spiritual ideas." Since God was a key reference point, she could not restrain herself from making that comment to Helena's ex-employers.

"Maybe voodoo influence. She's Haitian. She is also a devout Christian. Don't argue the point. She is a true believer. But you better toe the line. She will leave you if you don't. Heed her. She is a martinet, but in the end, you will have a clear conscience that you have done the best for your loved one. Believe me, dealing with this is a bitch, the worst. Be prepared. I was committed in my heart and mind not to let my spouse die in the hands of strangers."

While Helena rarely revealed the specific facts of her early life in Haiti, she was not shy about what she believed about the human condition, derived admittedly from her devotion to both voodoo and Roman Catholicism.

"We are all merely spirits who never die, and God decrees that we must help each other from one world to the next. Your husband's consciousness wants to enter the next phase of his perpetual life. If you want to keep him with you until he is truly ready to enter this phase, you must work hard to keep him here. Sooner or later, his mind will tell you when he is ready."

"Meaning?"

"It will go completely dark. And his spirit will be elsewhere."

Mumbo jumbo, Sarah had declared to herself, although she did obey Helena's so-called instructions designed to keep Frank "here." Helena's strategy was for Sarah to resist Frank's entry into his next phase by offering constant and repetitive reminders of past events of their long life together as well as prompting him to recall the subject that he had taught for so many years. She had militantly prescribed such memory-prompting dialogues and actually monitored Sarah's compliance.

So far, everything Helena's former employers said had been fulfilled, and Sarah was determined to keep her to the end.

"Bonjour, Madame," Helena said in her precise business-like English with a strong trace of singsong patois always spiced with a touch of sarcasm. She rode herd on Sarah's punctuality. As Sarah had been forewarned, Helena had strong views on the conduct required by loved ones. Her former employers had been honest in their evaluation.

In time, Helena's prescription had become routine, and Sarah obediently followed her instructions out of hope and fear—hope that it might be helpful in actually keeping Frank "here" and fear that if Sarah did not adhere to the routine, Helena would abandon them.

Their morning routine was written in stone. It took a couple of hours to get Frank ready to face the day. While Sarah took Shaina out for his morning walks, Helena did her caretaking chores. She bathed her patient, dressed him, sat him in front of the television in the living room, put on Turner Classic Movies, and set up the breakfast things on a portable table.

She prepared oatmeal, bananas, toast, and coffee for both Frank and Sarah, timed to Sarah's return so she and Frank could have breakfast together.

Sarah's daily role, especially during breakfast when Frank was comparatively more alert, was, following Helena's precepts, to reminisce, interrogate, recall details of their past lives hoping to jog a memory of past events and pushing Frank to reach deeply into his and their past. Sarah knew it defied all scientific state-of-the-art explorations of the human brain, but nevertheless, she pursued the possibility that what was tangled among the so-called synapses might untangle through sheer will and yet undiscovered scientific mysteries.

She dug deeply into her own memory to recall events in their lives, travel experiences, bringing up their children, reminding him about past travels, especially to the famous battlefields of the Civil War, his special interest.

She called up numerous references to politics, old friendships, humorous incidents, and whatever else might jog a remembrance. It was increasingly difficult to get a response, but she soldiered on despite discouragement and an increasing evidence of futility.

Helena, as the careful review of her references attested, had considerable experience with demented patients. Some of them had actually confirmed that Helena's prescriptions had extended the patient's clarity, although in the end, all had succumbed to the dark hole and eventual death. Nevertheless, all had agreed that Helena's ministrations were invaluable and eased the frustration and uncertainty for their loved ones. They had cited, too, that although Helena could be rigid and aggressively militant, she was a true find and Sarah was lucky to have discovered her.

Helena had prescribed a strict schedule that provided Frank with necessary certainty and a predictable routine, a tactic that kept him reasonably expectant and calm. Any variation confused and agitated him. Helena insisted that Sarah conform to the regimen and fulfill her commitment. When Sarah, for whatever reason, missed the exactitude of the schedule, as sometimes happened, she suffered days of Helena's scornful silent treatment.

Helena had been with them a year and had become increasingly assertive, arrogant, and bossy, but absolutely essential to Sarah's being able to cope with her failing husband. Sarah rarely contradicted Helena, although there were moments of rebellion, followed by guilt, anxiety, fear, and regrets on Sarah's part.

Helena was the fourth caretaker Sarah had hired in the past two years but the only one who could claim such highly specialized knowledge and experience with people suffering from Frank's condition. She worked six days a week and those evenings when Sarah was involved with various events connected to her causes, which ebbed and flowed according to whatever the current outrage was. She was now in the throes of advocating against any further military involvement in foreign wars, particularly Iraq and Afghanistan.

On Sundays, Helena's day off, a cousin of Helena's, inculcated with the same beliefs and tutored to follow Helena's rules, would provide backup assistance. Caring for Frank was growing increasingly difficult, especially at night when Sarah was the lone caretaker. At some point, she speculated, Frank would need Helena's full-time day and night care, which would entail turning Frank's study into a second bedroom. Helena had committed herself to the additional care when the time came. It would, of course, require a considerable increase of her fee.

Utilizing Helena's services was already extremely expensive, far, far beyond what Medicare and their supplementary policies would pay, and since Sarah had given up her law practice, the well-cushioned lifestyle that they had been living was beginning to become indeterminate. It was not yet dire, but the financial prospect was ominous as their once ample nest egg was shrinking precipitously.

Nevertheless, as Sarah had vowed, Frank was going to die in dignity in their home. Anything less would be a betrayal of her ideals.

They had Frank's pension and their two-bedroom condo, which could fetch a handsome price. She had rearranged their bedroom, adding a hospital-type bed and placing it beside the queen-sized bed on which Sarah slept, making her available to minister to Frank's needs during the night.

She often had to take Frank to the bathroom during the night, which played havoc with Sarah's and Shaina's sleep patterns since the white poodle slept on top of Sarah's bed beside her feet. She had always slept there, even when Sarah and Frank had slept together, and she did not change this habit when Frank was transferred to a single bed beside the marriage bed.

Sarah dismissed the nightly hardship as a necessary aspect of her sacrifice to be endured without complaint. She had no doubt that Frank would have done the same for her if the circumstances were reversed.

Nevertheless, Frank's unknown longevity, the chipping away of their savings, and the rising cost of the endgame when all factors were considered often added to Sarah's anxiety. Above all, she would never wish to be beholden to her children for support, especially Sheila, whom she often referred to as her Scarsdale daughter.

Sarah kissed Frank on his forehead. He nodded with a tiny tentative half-smile, never taking his eyes off the television screen.

"He's had his meds and a bath," Helena said in her French-flavored perfect English, which seemed to add more bite to her orders.

"Great," Sarah said. Frank loved his baths, and Sarah knew why. Helena's experience with older people in the hospice where she had worked was an invaluable asset. It wasn't compassion on her part. More like a professional understanding of what made older people, especially men, reasonably content.

Helena resented any interference or criticism, especially by Sarah, who knew full well that she was being kept captive by the Haitian. The fact was that anything Helena did to keep Frank content and cared for was worth whatever arrogance Sarah had to contend with.

"Anything that makes him happy, Helena," was Sarah's mantra. Perhaps, she decided, familiarity had the opposite effect on someone with Frank's affliction.

In the first years of their marriage, Frank had been an ardent sex partner, but that had tapered off in time, and Sarah had valiantly practiced every trick in her vast sexual inventory to keep him interested. As she aged, she was somewhat surprised that her sexual nature continued to maintain its strong influence over her mind and body, and her fantasies actually seemed to grow stronger and more vivid, and she reveled in them.

She did have the experience of two brief marriages before Frank and countless lovers, and she was an eager and adventurous participant. In each of her marriages, the sexual component had been primary at the beginning until she had discovered that loyalty, character, and kindness were not necessarily in proportion to the lavishly excessive male sex drive.

Despite this rocky early history, she had no regrets. She had lived a wild dream. There were no restraints. Looking back, she had become the quintessential hippie with an open sesame to drugs and every sexual license available. She did it all. It was one massive no-holds-barred orgy, and she had loved every minute of it.

And then the days of joyous excess slowly petered out, and she never failed to giggle when the pun reverberated in her mind. Responsibility had intruded. It was as if some invisible force had constructed a stop sign.

Her first husband had never moved past his teenage hippie years and was now an alcoholic, balding and overweight. His son—not *their* son—had sent her a computer photo of his father and informed her that he was living out his days in a hospice in Hawaii. Thankfully, they had had no children together.

Her second husband, with whom she was also childless, apparently had become a high school teacher who had married three more times and had numerous children. Years ago, he had written her a letter of apology for his conduct during their one-year marriage. She had long ago forgotten the specific cause of the ruptured relationship, nor did she care. At this time in her life, he seemed a vague apparition without substance, a ghost.

Somehow, her constitution had withstood the excess. She had been on a multiyear high in San Francisco, the locus of her youth. She had sown her oats thousands of miles away from her very traditional Orthodox Jewish parents who would have, in the parlance of her adolescence, had a shit conniption if they knew the real story of her early life. She told them she was out West studying to be a dental technician.

Oddly, in terms of her own daughters' upbringing, she had embraced many of her parents' conservative ideas and rules of conduct, although she doubted her daughters followed them. Youth, she had learned through her own experience, was remarkably creative in hoarding secrets from discovery by any elders.

She was 30 when she met Frank. He was Jewish, of a similar background, and helped her rejoin the ordered world of the mainstream strivers and find other ways to channel her considerable energy. The hippie manifesto of absolute unfettered freedom had morphed into a more structured pattern. She continued to consider herself a soldier in the army of do-gooders and super-savers of the world, liberals with an agenda of wrongs to be righted that stretched into infinity. She continued to enlist enthusiastically in the causes they spawned, although her participation was considerably constricted by her present circumstances.

To compensate for the cooling fires of her otherwise satisfying marriage with Frank, she did allow herself some loosening of the marriage bond, mostly on business trips out of town, sometimes with her clients, a dangerous and very unethical act for a lawyer. Still, she did not consider these acts as betrayal, but rather merely random recreation, and anyway, she felt certain that Frank might have dallied with a student or colleague under a similar definition. It had never ruffled their marriage or sense of togetherness.

She had been exceedingly discreet and careful and never

allowed any of these liaisons to go beyond a roll in the hay. She was certain that Frank did not dwell on such a possibility. Perhaps it was a silent pact between them. In time, his libido had waned to the point where her most strenuous ministrations had less and less effect, despite medicinal help. She had been told that lack of desire was one of the earliest symptoms of dementia.

Admittedly, her very furtive and occasional extramarital episodes were often impaired by guilt, which at times transcended her desire and often dampened the full enjoyment of these experiences. Worse, she deeply respected her husband and could not abide the possibility of humiliating him by exposure, and the thought of her daughters finding out compounded her fear of discovery. She felt certain that if Frank had stepped out of line, he too would have felt exactly the same way.

She had two daughters. Her oldest, Sheila, was, as it always seemed, somewhere in Africa. She had dedicated most of her life to, as she put it, helping the human underdogs. Exposed to her parents' compassionate liberalism from birth, she decided to take it one step further by actually entering the fray against poverty and disease with the total dedication and commitment of her physical presence.

She had a degree in nursing and would often volunteer in disease-ridden countries to assist Doctors without Borders or United Nations programs to shelter refugees from displacement. Often, she was unreachable for months at a time, although she managed to write occasional letters filled with descriptions of the horrors she was witnessing. On the very rare occasions when she resurfaced, Sheila would rail against the lip-service do-gooders who talked a good game but never put their lives on the line as she was doing. Sarah had no illusions about where the knife of criticism was pointed, but she never took the bait. She outwardly supported her daughter's sacrificing her life for the underdog, praising her lavishly for her work.

Inwardly, however, Sarah was more conflicted than supportive. Sheila's save-the-world focus had totally destroyed any family bonding, and as time went on and her long absences became the norm, the obligations of that relationship became merely sentimental nostalgia for both daughter and parents. For Sheila, her father's decline had become a mere detail to be asked about and noted, but it seemed to hold far less interest than her involvement in the sad spectacle of man's inhumanity.

Early on, Sheila had briefly married and quickly divorced when her husband caught on to the fact that her passions were more general than specific. There apparently were many lovers but no progeny.

Sarah was much closer to her second daughter, Charleen, a lesbian, who insisted on being addressed as Charley. She lived in Jackson Hole, Wyoming, where she was a ski instructor in the winter and a horse wrangler during the summer.

Sarah had shown understanding and acceptance of her daughter's sexual orientation, although under this façade was her preference for otherwise.

Growing up, both her daughters had been more affectionate with their gentle, scholarly father, far more, she knew, than with their demanding mother who had been the disciplinarian and scolder, determined that they would not replicate the wild abandon of her own youth, which became a subject of family lore.

Many of the friends she had kept in touch with from those days had died in early middle age, leaving her to wonder if their youthful lifestyle of sex, drugs, and other excesses had seriously impacted their longevity. Although she tried to represent that part of her life as a cautionary tale, she realized, perhaps too late, that it might have played a large role in both of her daughters' life choices.

When Frank became afflicted, her daughters were sympathetic, although Sheila was always too remote and busy to visit, and, of course, Charley lived too far away, although she did visit for a week once a year. Nevertheless, Sarah stubbornly resisted any temptation to be judgmental. That was, after all, one of the strongest pillars of her personal philosophy. Wasn't it?

Lately, Sarah had encountered a powerful enemy, a first-class unrelenting inhibitor: the aging process. It gradually informed her that most things in the human condition, even worse than those that motivated her political convictions, were unfair and unequal. One size, like socks, did not fit all. Frank, for example, was aging at lightning speed toward the dark icy winter of death, while she was still in the full maturity of early autumn, or even more accurately, late spring. The idea of it considerably and secretly undermined her lifelong obsession with so-called equality.

Their family doctor's best guess was that Frank would linger, perhaps for a year, maybe two, and become increasingly frail and completely unable to communicate or care for himself. Such a prospect did not inhibit Sarah's resolve to follow Helena's various memory-enhancing prescriptions, despite the frustration and ultimate failure, and to keep Frank at home until the end.

On that score, she was already scarred by her own experience with her mother, whom she had shipped off to a nursing facility against her will. Her mother had lasted exactly three days in the home, dying of, Sarah was certain, the sudden shock of separation. The guilt of that experience stayed with her and, in a strange way, further ennobled the sacrifice she was making.

And yet, here she was, still in good physical and mental health, which she attributed to pure luck, although she hedged her bets by actively participating in her twice-weekly yoga classes, her long walks with Shaina, her attendance at lectures at the 92nd Street Y, her vocal activism, and her healthy eating habits.

Although she could not compare her activism with Sheila's, she was a committed core-principled liberal, a first-class hater of anything that smacked of right wing, Republican, or conservative thinking. She was an outspoken feminist, a pro-choice evangelist, an anti-war fanatic, an inveterate protestor ready and willing to lift a banner or a placard that screamed the message that articulated her moral fervor. She was a fearless questioner of the power elite, a challenging ranter. She had marched with Martin Luther King Jr. and in any anti-Vietnam war protest available at the time. Jane Fonda had been her heroine. As a lawyer, Sarah had defended pro bono anyone she felt was trapped, as she characterized it, in the snare of injustice.

A great part of her energy these days was her pro-Israel stance and her fears about rising anti-Semitism in Europe and on college campuses. She admitted that her leftist views were often in conflict with Israel's policies, but despite this conflict, she was a dyed-in-the-wool Zionist and was fearful that anti-Semitism would one day rise in the United States. She strongly believed that the longer anti-Semitism was dormant, the stronger it would return.

Although she was not religious, she felt Jewish to the core and generally was wary and distrustful of non-Jews and overly sensitive to their alleged support of Israel and their oft spoken pro-Jewish sentiments. She was baffled and angry that the lesson of the Holocaust was fading and no longer the never-again object lesson it once was.

Yet she continued to cling nostalgically to the liberal mantra that humans were all one family and to love one another was the panacea for the future. Subsequent events were challenging that view, although she continued, even as she aged, to think of herself as a committed liberal.

Indeed, she had a lot of hash marks from her '60s experiences. While she had indulged freely in drugs and alcohol, a substance intolerance had saved her from debilitating consequences.

As for sex in those days, she was a greedy advocate and couldn't get enough of it.

Of course, despite her lucky avoidance of physical damage, her mental outlook as her time of excess wore on began to assail her with debilitating side effects. Withdrawal from such conduct pushed her into depression and a sense of loss and emptiness. She felt herself spiraling downward, uncertain of her future, lacking motivation, joyless, sinking into despair. Then came Frank.

Frank dropped into her life as if he had parachuted from heaven and landed beside her on a bench in Washington Square Park in lower Manhattan. As far as she can remember, she was certain that at the time, she was disoriented, depressed, and perhaps suicidal, a condition of intent that she admittedly might have fantasized.

Apparently, Frank was reading student papers he had extracted from an overstuffed briefcase. Conversation began. Sarah felt certain she had spoken first, although there had always been a debate between them about that.

They would characterize it as a case of random selection propelled by this mysterious mini-second of contact between them at exactly the right moment. They were destined to spend a lifetime assessing this moment. How come? Why them? What inner spark had blazed simultaneously in each of them?

More than 50 years had grown out of that rooted moment, 50 plus years of joint living, shared views on most issues, facing together pain, joy, anxiety, worry, confidence, child-making, child-rearing, and all the bonding and interaction that go with marriage and all its secrets, arguments, and conflicts. Such longevity, she swore, demands a special kind of fidelity encapsulated in the marriage vows about sickness and health and till death do us part.

Faced with the fulfillment of that pledge, Sarah had chosen obedience to its purpose and was determined to keep it as an iron clad commitment.

As she aged, especially in recent years, she labeled her recall and embellished sexual fantasies as her secret life, happily surprised that they had maintained their vigor for so long.

The prospect that she might become debilitated and no longer able to personally supervise Frank's last years was complicated and terrifying to her.

And then, of course, there was the immutable fact that a woman in her 80s, however well preserved, was not exactly a sexual target for the opposite gender under any conditions. It was not, as some suggested to take the onus off the reality, only a number. She would acknowledge frequently these days that 80 was fucking old age, and no amount of sugary bullshit could coat that reality.

Despite her early eager embrace of what was once called the hippie lifestyle, she had miraculously escaped any physical or mental complications, and both her early marriages took no toll on her psyche. Thankfully, both she and Frank had been perfectly in sync politically and socially. Nor did she have any doubts about their liberal positions. Both were irrevocably committed to them.

She had not expected her partner of more than 50 years to falter first, although she did know that the male lifespan statistics foretold an earlier demise. And now, in an odd way, that man she had just met at the East Side dog meadow had intrigued her. She figured him for the mid-70s, although the mathematics of his recall told her otherwise.

On closer observation, an instinctive evaluation based on his looks, his aura, and a lifetime of personal, tribally inspired bias suggested that he was some right wing East Side son of a bitch, a typical wasp goy who probably hated

Jews, Blacks, and Hispanics. Despite the emotional irrationality of her observation, she trusted her sixth sense about such stubborn conclusions.

Besides, with his fair skin, perfect profile, and general demeanor, she had little doubt that he harbored a foreskin in his undies pouch. Not that it ever mattered as a working instrument. She was very familiar with its operation. And yet to her surprise, she admitted to herself that he had engaged her in some strange and very confusing way. Perhaps it was simply that he amused her, or it might have been the coincidence of their matching dog breeds, or his somewhat formal flirtation that flattered and intrigued her.

It had been a long, long time since anyone, of whatever age, had flirted with her. She was, let's face it, an old biddy. She felt certain that it was utterly impossible for him to see her as a viable woman in any way. And yet, despite her misgivings, he actually made her feel like one.

She wondered why she could not dismiss him from her mind. The memory of his persona lingered in her thoughts. It was ridiculous that she should even give it a second thought, and she determined that she would avoid any further encounter and desist from taking the long walk to the East Side designated dog run.

The next morning, she very nearly broke her promise to herself not to go to the East Side and instead brought Shaina to Sheep Meadow on 68th street, where she had taken her when she was a puppy. She had not befriended any of the locals who represented an ever-rotating group, including many of the various celebrities that lived on the West Side. She had often chatted with the late actress Lauren Bacall who was a long-time West Sider, born and bred.

Her comment about the East Side having a better class of dogs was embarrassing now. Besides, it wasn't true. She chuckled to herself at her characterization and acknowledged that she missed Ben Franklin's parent and allowed herself to believe that Shaina missed Ben as well. For some reason, she began to feel a mysterious sense of absence but refused to classify it.

It classified itself when she saw Ben suddenly appear, and coming toward her was Harvey, a big smile pasted on his face.

"Ben insisted," he said coming up beside her.

"I hadn't realized Cupid's effect on the canine species." She giggled like a young girl, feeling genuinely happy to see him. Actually, she now determined that he was fairly handsome for a shkutz, a male goy.

"I admit I was a little concerned," he said with a wink, "that my East Side passport wouldn't let me through the gate. But I am relieved and thankful for the complete lack of discrimination."

Sarah giggled with teenage enthusiasm.

"You are a character, Harvey." Their gaze met and held for an uncommonly long moment. "I don't mean it as an insult."

"Nor did I take it as such," Harvey admitted, meeting her gaze again. He shrugged. "Maybe I just missed Shaina's parent."

"That again," she said, secretly pleased.

"What again?"

"You're flirting."

"Guilty as charged."

"That's a pretty bold assertion," she bantered, loving the byplay, forgetting the number that designated her age. Inspecting his face, she did acknowledge that despite the inevitable aging giveaways, he did look much younger. He had good skin, rosy cheeked from the morning chill, and he was quite tall with no sign of an old man posture. Nevertheless, she was baffled by his interest in her, an over-the-hill broken-down broad of 80.

Act your age, lady, she berated herself, yet she was secretly pleased. She wondered how many women of her age were thinking such thoughts. Not many, she decided with a certain pride. Concluding the fantasy, she hoped that if she was ever viewed in her natural state, the lights would be considerably dimmed.

After a few moments of rolling such errant speculations through her mind, she allowed herself to come down to earth. Harvey was speaking.

"I just thought you might be open to being friended, as the Facebook addicts contend."

"That's not friendship," she said. "That's FOMO."

"FOMO?"

"Fear of missing out," she explained. A young woman in her yoga class had used the term. Harvey seemed puzzled, and she confessed where she had heard the term.

"Out of my radar range," he admitted. Again, their gazes locked. "I'm not afraid of missing out. Not now."

My God, she thought, this old bird is really coming on to me. She felt confused but flattered. They watched their dogs sniffing each other.

"I always regretted having her spayed," Sarah mused aloud.

"Wouldn't matter now. I never did fix old Ben."

"Such generosity."

"He used to get fidgety around bitches in heat."

"Can't fight Mother Nature."

"I was never sure I did him a favor. As far as I know, he had no progeny."

"He might have sneaked in an affair or two." She winked, giggled, and shrugged. The talk was suggestive, and she felt a tiny shiver of sexual excitement.

Obviously avoiding further discussion on the subject, Harvey looked around, inspecting the area.

"Dog lovers are the same everywhere," he said. "Guess both us and them have this need for absolute devotion."

"Ah! A philosopher," she noted with a chuckle. "But then we are on the West Side, which is also ground zero for philosophers, most of them of my religious persuasion."

He laughed.

"You're really hung up on that idea," he said with mild admonishment.

"Maybe," she admitted. Then a sudden thought intruded. "You know, Oppenheimer went to the Ethical Culture School just down the street." She pointed with her chin. Perhaps it was a veiled reference to Jews.

"Now that's an odd thought."

"I think of that event every time I pass that building. The bomb."

"That was years ago. Maybe before you were born."

She looked at him archly, warmed by the compliment. She smiled and shook her head.

"They should not have dropped that bomb on Japan," she said. "Killing all those people."

"It prevented the potential murder of thousands, perhaps millions of Japanese and Americans."

"Yes, that is the right wing version."

"The historic conclusion," he began and then stopped, cautious suddenly. "Why suddenly are you thinking about Oppenheimer?"

"I couldn't help myself," Sarah admitted, shrugging. "Maybe I was making a point."

"What point was that?"

"The Ethical Culture School building is a prominent feature of my neighborhood. Maybe I was making amends. You know, showing that East Side, West Side, both sides have the good and the bad. Proves my remarks yesterday were a bubbameister. "

"Another yiddishism?"

"Means a bullshit story."

She felt flustered. What's going on with me? This guy is

having a weird affect. This was not the time to conjure up political challenges. Had his look and persona presented a tempting political target? Her remarks, she decided, were inappropriate for the moment, a spoiler.

"Let's not go there," she sighed, absolutely certain that would be his choice as well.

"I hadn't intended to."

She felt embarrassed and thought he must think she's a flake. Suddenly, she looked at her watch.

"Nearly time," she said.

"I was hoping we might have coffee."

She looked at her watch again. Helena was with Frank, and a break in routine always set off Frank's anxiety and upset him. She would miss the ritual breakfast, which would set off Helena's fury and agitate Frank. She felt constricted, trapped. No, she decided, I am still viable. I do not want to miss this, whatever it portended.

"I'm sort of expected," she said, feeling the pull of the invitation and his quite obvious eagerness. And hers.

"To tell you the truth, I'd like to get to know you better."

"I'm not averse to that," she replied. "Really, but I...I have this previous commitment." She looked at her watch again. "I'm so sorry."

"Some other time then," he said shrugging, clearly disappointed.

"Sure," she said, feeling a sudden surge of regret. They signaled for their dogs, who obediently came toward them so they could hook up their leashes. Harvey, sporting a clear expression of disappointment, waved a tepid goodbye and began to move away. Sarah felt strongly conflicted. Then pulling out her cell phone, she punched in Helena's number. Helena answered in her perpetual tone of annoyance.

"I'm going to be late today, Helena."

"He is going to be a problem."

"It can't be helped, Helena," she said firmly. "It's too confining. Really, Helena. I can't always be there."

"You know how he gets." She deliberately seemed to be avoiding the obvious, her original commitment.

"Yes, I do, but sometimes. Tell him I'm getting him some chocolate ice cream for later."

For Frank, ice cream could be a placating food, especially chocolate. She couldn't think of anything else.

"We have plenty of chocolate ice cream in the fridge."

"He doesn't know that," Sarah snapped, sensing an argument coming on.

"This is not a good idea."

"Okay then, give him a bath."

"He had his bath."

"Then give him another one," Sarah shot back, feeling churlish.

At times, Helena's tactic was silence, especially when she was angry. Conflicted and uncertain, Sarah said, "Just make do for Christ's sake, Helena. I'll be home as soon as I can." She hoped she had pulled back from the brink.

There was no response from Helena, and Sarah hung up in exasperation. Bitch, she mumbled as she hurried after Harvey. Helena was always a bundle of resentment and hated being second guessed. One way or another, Sarah would either pay the price for this or lose her, which would be a disaster. She pushed the thought from her mind.

"Harvey!" she called as she hurried after him. He was just out of earshot, but she followed him swiftly, catching up.

"I know a place," she said breathlessly. He turned and looked at her with some confusion. "We'll have to sit outside. There's a Starbucks, but it's always jammed and not exactly dog friendly."

"I'm delighted," Harvey said, his expression brightening.

"You might say I acquired a case of FOMO," she said,

suddenly conscious that she was reacting positively to his flirtation.

She led him west to Broadway where she knew a hole-in-the-wall shop where they could get coffee, and then she led him to a tiny outdoor pocket park. It was comfortable, and the sun had warmed the metal benches.

"Good idea," Harvey said.

The dogs had both settled quietly beside the bench while they continued to hold on to their leashes. Strangely, a wall of awkwardness had arisen, driving them both to silence. She couldn't understand it, especially his sudden shyness after being more than forward and flirtatious. But she, too, was cautious, knowing that any wrong moves, like the stupid reference she had made about the Ethical Culture School might curtail any further possibilities of friendship between them. She searched her mind for some neutral starting point and then hit upon the obvious, exchanging life statistics.

"You don't sound like a native New Yorker," she said. "But then from the looks of you, that's pretty obvious."

He laughed and seemed pleased by the contorted question, perhaps relieved.

"I thought I had lost the twang. But you got it right. I'm from the wilds of the Midwest. Kansas. Ever been?"

"Never. Off the beaten track for me."

"You're not alone. Salt of the earth people, though I knew I had to come to the Big Apple to make my fortune."

"And did you?"

"I give myself a B. Good job. Creative director at a big ad agency. Didn't get to the top spot, but no regrets. Good marriage. One son, lives in London. A number of grandchildren. Don't see much of them these days. Wife died years ago. I think I mentioned that. That's my stats. It's me and Ben now, but then you know that."

He was fumfering, she thought. She had already done

that. They locked eyes again, and she felt a thrill of magnetism that she acknowledged only to herself. She knew he was waiting for a response.

"You?" he prodded.

She found herself debating a response and for some reason feared the truth might inhibit their future. Future? She was puzzled by the reference. Hadn't she already implied that?

"Widow," she lied.

His eyes brightened with encouragement. She immediately admonished herself. How could she be so callous as to tell such a whopper? But then she had calculated that an admission that she was married, whatever the circumstances, might complicate a possible relationship.

She was being ridiculous, she knew. What was the point at her age? Yet here she was, participating in flirtation, a situation she had not experienced in decades. Worse, she felt certain that he represented everything she opposed politically and culturally. She had adopted the lies of a cheat, offering an open sesame to a relationship that would be more in line for a much younger spouse bent on adultery. Worse, she now feared that a quick admission might give him pause in his pursuit. She let the lie persist.

"A long marriage?"

"Very," she agreed, pressing forward. At least that part was the truth.

"Happy?"

"Like yours, I guess."

"Still practicing law?"

"A time to hold. A time to fold," she said. "I folded. Had enough."

Another lie, she thought. She hadn't had enough. She had Frank to care for.

She pondered a follow-up, mostly to get ahead of the lies and wander on to other topics. Actually she had long forgotten how these flirtations were pursued, although she found herself excited about where it might lead. He sipped his coffee and surveyed the area. There were no other people around.

He nodded toward Shaina.

"You bring her to the park every day?"

"Rain or shine. Like you and Ben here. It's a ritual." It had only been her ritual when Frank could no longer comply. Another lie? Perhaps a white one.

"Absolutely. We rarely miss a morning. Except maybe if there's a heavy rain or a blizzard."

She nodded, her thoughts racing now, suddenly committed to keeping this relationship going come what may.

"Neither do we."

"Mostly on the West Side?" he asked.

"Always. I guess yesterday I just felt like trying something different." At times, she felt overwhelmed with burdens and felt the need for a change of landscape.

"Lucky me."

She leaned her head back and laughed. "Your line is so old fashioned."

"I guess I am as old fashioned as one gets."

"This is ridiculous, you know. At our age."

"Ridiculous? I would say fortuitous," Harvey said. "Not often does one meet such an attractive person of serious interest."

"Serious interest. Wow!"

"Things happen."

"You're pulling my leg, Harvey," she laughed, feeling the years peel away, forgetting her lies for the moment and then actually compounding them.

"Yes, they do," she added.

"Why not? We're free, white, and over 21."

"Way over," she said.

"I didn't ask."

"I didn't tell."

Despite her reluctance to admit her age, she was contemplating yet another lie. At some point, she decided, she would shave maybe five years or more. Seventy-five seemed logical. She felt certain she could pass for that unless he snatched her wallet and saw her driver's license.

"That free white part sounds racist," she said as a reflex, then regretted it. The statement reflected the original lie. She was hardly free in the way he meant it. Instead, she again surrendered to the ever multiplying string of deceptions.

"I hadn't meant it that way," he said apologetically. "Guess I'm stuck with the old clichés."

Nevertheless, it sounded waspy, and she was tempted to make some pithy rebuttal but checked herself. Such a response at this moment was clearly knee-jerk and irrelevant.

"Guess so." Once again she was conscious of the lie extending itself, becoming the norm.

"I'd like to see you again, Sarah. Why stand on pretense at our age? I admit it. I'm attracted to you." He smiled and winked.

"My God! Harvey is a fast worker," she giggled, noting again that it seemed like a young girl's giggle.

"I would be slower if I had more time. These days, time is at a premium."

"You can say that again," she sighed.

"I'd rather not."

"I agree," she said, nodding. She paused, and once again their eyes locked. "I admit I've thought about you, mostly because I judge us to be complete opposites." She was loving this.

"That's partially hopeful. I've heard that opposites attract."

"Attract arguments, you mean."

"Okay then, let's agree to disagree."

"I can't agree to that." She giggled again, enjoying the banter. She could not remember when she had bantered like this. "Most of the people I meet in my life every day agree with me."

"Then I must seem exotic."

Again she giggled. She could not remember when she had had so much fun. "You do. By God, you do."

"But I am open to adopting a different point of view."

"At your age? Hey, Harvey, now you're losing your authenticity."

"Does that mean you will never change your mind on anything?"

"It has never occurred to me. I am absolutely positively on the right side of history on most subjects, especially when it comes to politics and fairness and justice and decency and whatever." She laughed again.

"I love to see you laugh."

"Shit, Harvey. Now you're going too far. You're chatting me up for ulterior motives." She felt wonderful, open, happy, sexy. She noted physical signs. "I don't believe this conversation."

"Neither do I, but I'm happy it has taken this direction."

"You sure are an optimist."

"Yes, I am. Although," he paused, "my reach exceeds my grasp."

"Not bad, Harvey," she said with genuine admiration. This guy has all his marbles, she noted, thinking of poor Frank, his mind lost in a deep fog.

"I was, after all, a creative director."

"Now you're bragging," she said, not wanting to break the chain of what she thought was their snappy dialogue. For the first time in years, she felt enlivened, transfused.

"I'm trying to impress you."

"You're over that hurdle, Harvey," she said with another slight giggle.

He seemed to grow thoughtful suddenly. "Tell you the truth, Sarah. I don't know what's come over me. I feel like a kid pitching woo."

"Pitching woo? God, Harvey, you are something." Their eyes locked for a long moment. She felt the odd pressure of her quickening heartbeat. "This is utterly ridiculous, but I'm having fun. I admit it."

"So am I," Harvey acknowledged.

"People our age don't do this."

"Who said?"

He suddenly reached for her hand and lifted it to his lips. She let him, enjoying the clasp and feel of his flesh.

"This is beyond madness, Harvey."

"I know."

They fell into a kind of pregnant silence, their eyes locked.

"I have a plan," Harvey said, breaking the silence.

"Plan?"

"We alternate. I come west one day, and you come east the next."

His plan surprised her. What did he have in mind?

"Or if it suits you better, I can come west every day. It's longer, but the walk might do me good."

She grew thoughtful for a moment. Does this old goat want to get into my knickers? She studied his face and determined that his expression was loaded with sincerity. What was she thinking? He wanted to bring her to his own home turf and lure her to his apartment. She tried to picture it in her mind. The seduction! She felt her nipples harden. Was he really that confident that he could rise to the occasion? Or was it merely mind over matter? Pure bullshit, she decided, withdrawing her hand but willingly going along with this absurd fantasy.

"Sounds like a worthy plan," she said, despite her doubts.

"Then we could meet for coffee, chat for awhile. Like this. Of course, I wouldn't want to spoil your day. Actually, I never asked how you spend your time. You said you gave up your law practice. Divorce was your specialty. Are you consulting on that with other lawyers then?"

"Actually," she paused, not wanting the lies to expand. It was bad enough as it was. She had told enough lies for the day. "When a chapter is over, it's over. I do mostly pro bono on issues."

"Issues?"

"Civil rights. Climate change." She hesitated for a moment and studied his face. "Israel."

He nodded. "I'm with you on that one."

"Really?"

She immediately regretted the question. It revealed her inherent distrust of non-Jews on matters like Israel. Of course, she was always at war with her sense of tolerance. It hadn't mattered during her so-called wild years when Jews were still living under the spell of the Holocaust and being pro-Jew was a moral imperative. That attitude was generally disappearing, and the old hatreds were becoming more evident.

She noted how the battle lines were changing. More and more conservatives were pro Israel these days, although she was wary of that support. Her question seemed to have surfaced of its own accord, revealing the old fault line between Jew and Gentile. She quickly changed the subject.

"I'm one of those save-the-world people," she said, smiling broadly, thinking suddenly of her daughter and her obsessive mission.

"And how is the world doing?"

"Shitty," she replied. "Doesn't mean we should give up the battle."

"I'll settle for one good bang-up decade."

"And then?"

"Well," he chuckled, "after that, there will be no 'then'."

"So you're a pessimist."

"A realist." He silently studied her face for a long moment. She held his gaze and was beginning to feel a strange connection. "Tell you the truth, at this moment I feel like an optimist."

She caught his implication and suddenly felt guilt intrude. Poor Frank, she thought, surely upset by her absence. And here she was, flirting like a teenager with this stranger, telling him a pack of lies to make her look better in his eyes. She wondered where this was leading.

His eyes followed her as she looked at the watch on the inside of her wrist.

"I better get going."

She rose, and they moved together with their dogs in the direction of the park. Her apartment was just around the corner, and he walked her to the entrance. She felt suddenly panicked by the thought that he might have expected to be invited in. She turned to face him.

"It's been fun," she said.

He nodded and hesitated for a moment as they looked at each other. Something is going on, she acknowledged to herself.

"And the plan?" he said.

"The plan?" She knew what he meant but feigned forgetfulness. It seemed like a commitment, and she wasn't prepared for that. By then, her sense of guilt had expanded, and she began to think of the effect of her lateness on Frank. Suddenly, she felt deeply conflicted.

"I had made this suggestion," he began, perhaps noting by her expression a lack of commitment. She felt flustered, disoriented, unable to comprehend an answer.

"Tell you what," Harvey said. "I'll call in the morning. Let me have your cell phone number."

"Cell?"

She felt another lie surface. He looked puzzled by her apparent confusion. She let his request hang in the air. It frightened her. Too far, she thought, panicked now. She looked toward the entrance, suddenly anxious with what she was about to face upstairs. Thankfully, he didn't press the point. He reached into his back pocket, pulled out a wallet, and extracted a crumpled card.

"Mine is on here," he said. "You can confirm."

By then, her attention was compromised. I can't do this, she decided. In a robotic gesture she took the card and put it in the pocket of her jacket.

"I enjoyed the morning," she muttered, not offering her hand or a proper good-bye and leaving him speechless on the street. The doorman nodded, and she made her way through the lobby, dreading what she was about to face.

Maybe I've stumbled into the wrong playpen, she thought. Or not.

She put her key into the apartment lock.

-3-

Not only was Harvey baffled by Sarah's sudden departure, he was also concerned that he might have said or done something wrong. She had been so forthright, so interested, so engaged, and then suddenly she had retreated into a shell.

Perhaps he had offended her in some way. After all, they were eons apart in their political views, but hadn't they, at least in theory, agreed to disagree? He did not believe such differences were a bar to their relationship, or for that matter, any sincere relationship. People were prone to differ. So what?

She actually seemed to enjoy the give and take of their contrary views. Had she suddenly become hostile to him because of those views? Was he too flippant? Too serious?

Or was it something to do with the fact that he was not Jewish? Suddenly, he was reminded of Anne's bias, which led to speculation about how Sarah might have reacted if the situation were reversed and he was the Jew and Sarah was the Gentile. It would not have mattered to him one bit. People were people. Besides, at their age, why would it matter? In his version of the endgame, they were all headed to the same void.

Throughout the morning, Harvey continued to rack his brain to discover the source of what he sensed was a sudden cleavage. He could not understand it. For the first time in many years, he felt the debilitating power of rejection.

But why? What was so meaningful about this woman who moved him to this very oddly powerful emotional response? Why didn't she give him her cell phone number?

He had seen her use a cell phone. Why the refusal? But she did, after all, accept his card with his number on it. The test would be if she called, and it was too early to know what to expect.

He debated about canceling lunch at the Century with George Hapsworth but then decided it might take his mind off Sarah and the effect she was having on his tranquility. It seemed unseemly for a man his age to be going through such absurd angst and ridiculous expectations.

More than once during the remainder of the morning he peered at his cell phone screen with the vague hope that he might get a call or a text from Sarah. Finally, he decided to head to his lunch with George.

"See you later, alligator," he called out to Ben, who was slumbering on the living room floor. Ben stirred briefly and opened his eyes as if to acknowledge Harvey's departure and wave good-bye. Downstairs, Harvey nodded to the doorman as he left the building and took the bus to the clubhouse on 43rd street. Even the usual frenetic street activity could not shake the thoughts of Sarah from his mind. He was clearly distracted as he reviewed their morning conversation ad infinitum.

"Why so hangdog, Harv?" George asked as Harvey joined him in the dining room. George, who navigated with a walker, was already seated.

"Does it show?"

Harvey had known George for more than half a century. He had been a top account man at Y and R, and clients liked him because of his often reckless rants about the advertising business. "We are mammon's whores," he had sloganized regularly.

George loved to expound his theory of the "pleasure promise" as the basis for all advertising. It was his privately owned cliché, and defining it with gusto was mesmerizing and enormously persuasive to his fellow workers and clients. His presentation skills were legendary, his charisma powerful. In his prime, he was a serial womanizer, and he had lived through the wreck of four marriages and countless mistresses.

At 93, he had reached sage status and had lost little of his cynicism and ranting skills. Harvey still loved to listen to his often outrageous diatribes and looked forward to their bi-weekly lunches.

George had concocted an elaborate support system to carry him through to his demise. He was determined to spend down his wealth, amassed by shrewd market advice and insider tips from clients. He bragged about hoping he would end up with debt and obligations as his legacy for his unloved, unloving, and ungrateful progeny. On his payroll was a chauffeur, a full-time nurse, a live-in assistant, and numerous part-time others who served his lifestyle at his apartment in Waldorf Towers.

"My objective is to not lift a fucking finger to get through to the end," he recited like a mantra. He needed a walker and sometimes oxygen and remained undaunted by quadruple open-heart surgery, two hip replacements, one knee replacement, powerful hearing aids, and thick glasses to help him maneuver through his day. His mind was still razor sharp, his cynicism consistent, and his sense of humor intact. Although he was bone thin and his face cadaverous, alert piercing brown eyes that flashed over high cheekbones attested to the man's fierce and laser-like alertness.

Another issue at the top of his agenda was what he believed was the coming era of death committees where anonymous bureaucrats would decide at what age and health conditions the government would cease to pay for procedures to prolong life, and he was out to prove the lie to that inevitability by living as long as he could and by being the poster boy for opposition to that looming possibility.

George's sole outings consisted of lunch at the Century a

few times a month with former colleagues. He was a perfect recipient of confidences and dispensed wisdom and opinions as if they were pronouncements from God. His advice was often toxic and required a level of courage impossible for most people to muster.

To Harvey, George offered nostalgia for the career years, companionship, entertainment, and a primer for survival. At lunch, they always wrote down their orders, and the experienced old waiters who served them would bring them both the traditional silver goblets of dry martinis.

"The race goes on," George said, lifting his goblet for a small sip. "Me first or the planet?"

"From the gloomy news and my current perspective, I put my money on you, George. The planet is going to hell in a handbasket, and as of this moment, I feel totally fucked." Harvey raised his goblet and took a deep swig.

The goblet always contained a double, and for Harvey, that was no more than a once-a-week draught. George, however, maintained that his daily double martini lunch at the Century or elsewhere assured his longevity for another 24 hours.

They began their lunch conversation with a general sweep of the state of affairs, always critical of existing political leadership and the general condition of the world's economy and various growing antagonisms currently drawing blood among people and nations.

"Man in his naked state is an evil, predatory, ruthless son of a bitch. Bottom line. He cleverly disguises his sick nature with platitudes about progress and has set up a system that rewards power and greed above all. If only those fucking save-the-world morons would get it."

"Get what?" Harvey asked. He enjoyed goading George to go over the cliff in his assessment of the human race. Despite the perpetual harangue, there was always a smattering of truth in his pronouncements.

"The true nature of man," he said as he arranged his features as a sinister mask, "is predatory. He needs restraints to keep that true nature under control. In the absence of that, it is every man for himself."

"Women, too, George?"

"Especially women."

"I'll buy that," Harvey said, his agreement influenced by his present dilemma.

By the time their omelets arrived, the inevitable main dish that would be followed by the celebrated rice pudding, George's philosophical rants had sputtered, and they had exhausted current events and the dread they foretold.

After his early morning experience, which had morphed in his mind as a form of betrayal, Harvey felt some degree of comfort talking with a curmudgeon like George who offered part entertainment, part truth. The conversation in recent years was never complete without George going off on the subject of dying, which, considering his physical condition, was understandable.

"The idiot behind Obamacare has written this article about hoping to die at 75. His logic is impeccable. The body goes to shit beginning then. I had my first two stents put in at 75, a hint of what was to come." He smiled and lifted his goblet for another sip. "Look at me now. Eighteen years later. A bag of rotting flesh and bones. That man is not a fool." He chuckled, showing browned teeth. "Of course, that doesn't mean he is not an asshole." He tapped his temple. "This fucker stays in shape, and that's where the deceptive son of a bitch is dead wrong." He tapped his temple again. "If they had cut me short at 75, they would have deprived this organ of an 18-year run going for 20."

"Not everybody can boast about that organ surviving intact," Harvey said. "For some, the lights go out early."

"Granted. But there are other organs on the menu as well." He pointed to his eyes, his nose, and his mouth. One can still see some beautiful things in this fucked up world, at least for now. Movies. Sunrise. Sunsets. Paintings." He pointed to his nose. "I can still smell pleasant things. The earth. Flowers. Perfume. Even my own farts, which are rather comforting to sniff." He laughed. Then he pointed to his ears. "Sounds. Duly amplified by technology. Beautiful music, conversation, street sounds, the bloody annoying cacophony of city life." He waved his arm to encompass the dining room. "People, too. Always the living sounds of people." Then he stuck his finger to his mouth. "Speech." He took another small sip from his goblet. "Taste. They say the taste buds are the last to go. I still get a blast from my taste buds." He focused his fierce eyes on Harvey's face as if he were his chosen villain. "And who the fuck is that cocksucker to think it's all over at 75? Or 95? Or 100?" He took another deep sip of his martini. Harvey knew that one of his so-called major pronouncements was coming.

"We are not socks. One size does not fit all," he intoned. Odd, Harvey thought, having concocted the same image earlier, acknowledging its origins. He had merely recycled one of George's pronouncements.

"There are other parts that are not so lucky," Harvey said, offering what he knew was a tongue-in-cheek response.

"You are referring, of course, to the almighty cockadoodle."

"Among some other inner organs," Harvey said.

"Nonsense, my friend. The other organs are programmed to fail. It is the cockadoodle that is the real metric of the living male. When that fails, gender disintegrates and becomes merely historic. The cockadoodle is central to keeping the planet populated."

"I'll buy that," Harvey said, lifting his goblet for another sip. George winked, lifted his goblet, and tapped Harvey's.

For some reason, Harvey was thinking of Sarah and the outlines of her ample bust, which inflated her outerwear and gave promise of fleshly delights. Aside from that observation, he had not thought of Sarah in a strictly sexual sense. Until this moment. He felt a quickening sensation in his penis, a kind of prelude to an erection, which quickly subsided. Such a sensation always cleared away depressing thoughts. It was, he assured himself, a measure of his maleness, however faint the signal.

They set aside their goblets and began to eat their omelets. George was generous with the salt shaker. Harvey buttered a roll, and they ate for a few moments in silence. It suddenly occurred to Harvey that he could not recall a serious discussion about the penis with another non-medical man except in some jesting sexual reference or in the context of the drugs for erectile dysfunction. But even that latter discussion was skeletal and dealt only with efficacy in a technical sense.

"Tell me, George," Harvey said. "Do you still think about sex?"

He felt George's eyes focus on his face, which proceeded to react with a hot flush. George chuckled.

"Bet your biddy, Harvey. But there's a long jump from the thought to the act. I've had my share, more than my share. Believe me, Harvey, the thinking part never falters. As to the sensation." He grew thoughtful. "Comes and goes." He shrugged and offered a low chortle. "Not a pun."

"Does it ever rise to the occasion?"

George reacted with a cryptic smile. "Harvey, why the sudden interest?"

"The interest isn't sudden, George. The topic of conversation is."

George surveyed Harvey's face. "You're serious." It wasn't a question. More of a pronouncement.

Harvey hesitated. "I think so."

"I confess that it is the main topic of my nostalgia and the perpetual subject of my fantasies. Sex, to me, Harvey, is the pinnacle of my sensations. I love it. I seek it constantly. I have always been ravenous, with an enormous appetite. I knew the way to it, Harvey. I could sniff it out in a wink."

"Now you're bragging, George." Harvey was beginning to feel the martini's reaction. "Although I do note the present tense."

"Allow for some exaggeration," George huffed. "The past was my heyday. As for the present? Hell, batting averages decline."

"And yours?"

George grew thoughtful. "I can still bunt," he shrugged. "Big pharma offers help." Suddenly, he began to roar with laughter, and his eyes teared up.

"Seriously?" Harvey asked, as if sharing in George's joke.

"Do I require letters of reference?" George asked, wiping his eyes with a napkin.

"Only if the respondents are still alive to validate your reporting."

"Perhaps I should have videoed any recent performance as proof of my skill." Again, George offered a loud guffaw. He was having a good time.

Watching him, Harvey could imagine seeing his mind's gears shifting for an apt answer. He smiled and shrugged.

"I try my best to keep the soldier on the battlefield," George chuckled for a moment. "I have to call in reinforcements on occasion."

"You're talking in riddles, George."

"It is all a riddle," George sighed. "Perking up Peter is a losing game, I'm afraid. The law of diminishing returns rules. When I do hit a single occasionally, I am very grateful and usually tip the giver another hundred." He winked, drained his goblet and let out a laugh that caused the people at the nearby tables to look their way.

Harvey offered a polite chuckle.

"So you are still in the game?"

"Unfortunately they keep moving the goalposts," George said with a wink. "When that goes, the government can shovel me into the grave."

He laughed aloud again. This time, Harvey joined him and surveyed the diners.

"Do you think anyone of our demographic in this place is discussing this topic?"

"In our demographic, it is like background music. Always there even if we're not consciously listening. "

"George, you are always so fucking profound." Yes, Harvey thought. Since this morning I am suddenly hearing the music.

The lunch over, Harvey helped George rise and assisted him into a position behind his walker, and then they made their way to the elevator.

At the outside door, George's driver moved to help him into his car.

The two men shook hands, but before George moved away, he turned to Harvey and lifted his hand, pointing a finger. It was a kind of parting ritual.

"Here's the way to look at this last chapter, Harvey. Think of life as a toothpaste tube. When it gets down to the last drop of toothpaste, you roll up the tube, twist it, and squeeze to get that last drop of paste out of it. It's that last squeeze that is the hardest, and you're often tempted to toss away the tube. I say keep twisting, go for that last drop, because in the end, there's only you and that mouthful of teeth, if you have any left. Spare no effort. Polish up that smile. Don't leave a single drop in the tube. Get it? In the end, there is only you. So be good to yourself before the lights go out."

That thought in various incarnations was always George's parting shot. Harvey had heard the toothpaste tube metaphor before.

"I'm going to rush back and brush my teeth," Harvey said.

He walked the 20 odd blocks back to his apartment. In retrospect, the conversation's recall was comedic enough to prod him to laugh out loud. A passerby looked at him strangely.

The temperature was dropping, and the bright fall day was throwing dark shadows along the pavement. Lunch with George had lifted his spirits, but they were beginning to decline again as he grew closer to his apartment and began to think again of his morning rejection.

Ben, who spent most of his time these days napping, was always alert to the sound of Harvey's key in the lock and ready to greet him with as much energy as he could muster. Harvey fussed over him, knelt to cuddle him, and checked his water and food bowls.

Later, he took Ben out for what he hoped would be the last walk of the night. But the contagion of his own tossing and turning on Ben, who slept beside his bed, prompted Ben to react with equal turmoil, and Harvey found himself walking Ben across the street to the edge of the park for a mutual pee at two in the morning.

Later, suffering from nervous fatigue, Harvey was in his outdoor clothes at 5:00 a.m. walking Ben to his East Side rendezvous, releasing him on the dog lawn before any of the canine crew arrived. At that hour, the air was cold, and the dark, blank sky was a clear harbinger of rain.

There had been no call from Sarah, and Harvey spent the time looking into the dark western area of the park, an unfruitful exercise of searching for any sign of Sarah and Shaina. By 8:00, it was apparent that Sarah and Shaina were not coming, which prompted him to leash Ben and start the trek westward to the 79th Street West Side dog playground.

He admonished himself for his action. It would take at least 20 minutes to a half hour to cover the distance to the West Side at a fast pace. He speculated that he might be met with cold indifference. Worse, he was risking being totally ignored. The woman should at least have the courtesy to call him and resolve the situation. Resolve what? He repeated the notion to himself that he had absolutely no claim on her time or attention.

He was being irrational, stupid, and childish. In fact, he was out of control. Considering his age, he was embarrassed by his actions. Was he in the grip of some schoolboy crush? That latter thought sobered him, but not enough to stop his relentless movement westward.

Going forward, somewhat out of breath, noting that Ben was winded as well, he caught a glimpse of Shaina among the frolicking dogs. Oddly, his anxiety increased. How was he to approach her? Rebuke? Indifference? Casual? He was conflicted. Then, of all things, he felt fearful and debated turning back.

Before he could make up his mind, he caught Sarah's attention, who contrary to his expectations, waved enthusiastically and rushed forward to meet him. She knelt, patted Ben, and unleashed him.

"Go, Ben. She missed you."

They watched Ben move forward at a slow pace to join the group. Soon he was spotted by Shaina, who met him and began the sniffing routine.

"I'm sorry, Harvey," Sarah said. "I had meant to get in touch. Really."

"I was hoping you would, but you were under no obligation."

He was feigning indifference but wasn't sure she was buying it. After all, he had walked the long distance to the West Side.

"I just thought it was strange," he said. "We seemed to be getting along famously."

"Yes, we were."

Their eyes locked, and he felt his heartbeat accelerate. Then she turned away briefly. He noted that she took out a handkerchief, dabbed her eyes, and then turned again to face him.

"Tell you the truth, Harvey, it was a terrible morning. I was hoping you'd come."

He felt his heart jump. Still, he was totally confused by her remark.

"You could have called. I gave you my cell number."

"I know," she sighed. "I misplaced it."

"You did?" He was totally confused.

"It's a long story," she said, her voice catching.

"Anytime you're ready to tell it, I'm ready to listen."

She nodded but did not reply.

"I wished you would come, Harvey. Really." She hesitated for a moment, and he sensed she wanted to say more. After a moment, she appeared to reject the idea. Their eyes locked again, and she smiled broadly. Like a coquettish young woman, she whispered, "Will you forgive me?"

Good God, he thought, for it was at that moment that he realized something had occurred in him that seemed dredged up from long ago, as if he had suddenly found himself as another person, younger, oddly awkward with the curious realization that he might be in love. In a bold, seemingly courageous act, he reached out for her hand and brought it up to his lips.

"Apology accepted."

They held hands now, standing side-by-side in silence watching their dogs at play.

"I'm so happy you came, Harvey." She squeezed his hand, and he felt its strength. He hoped it was sincere and wondered what she meant when she said, "It's a long story."

The other dog parents signaled that the time was up by leashing their charges. Harvey noted that Sarah seemed to hesitate while she clung to his hand.

"Coffee time, Sarah?"

She released his hand, leashed Shaina, and then looked up at Harvey.

"Not today, Harvey." Then she stood up and looked at her watch.

"Now I'm a bit confused, Sarah."

"I know."

"We could sit in that little park and talk, like before." There was no way she could mistake the pleading in his voice.

"I can't, Harvey. I'm sorry. I have, well, I have a regular appointment." She looked at her watch again. "I just can't be late."

He nodded, confused and trying to rationalize her excuse. After all, she hadn't expected him and must have made other plans.

"Later perhaps? You set the time. I'm free." He avoided the free, white, and 21 reference, but surely she must have remembered it.

"Walk with me to my apartment building, Harvey." Their eyes locked again, and he detected some sudden tears. She reached into her pocket and took out a tissue. With both dogs leashed, they walked along a park path to the park exit near her building.

Harvey was clearly troubled. Of all the people in his world, he wanted to be with Sarah. He was determined not to over analyze his sudden attraction, although he was baffled by the intensity. Why this woman? He glanced toward her as they walked, trying to read her face, her expression, what she might be thinking.

She must have sensed his keen interest and turned his way, offering a smile. He could feel the mutuality, the power of this strange magnetism. They rearranged their grips on their dogs' leashes and reached out to hold hands. Her grip was strong as she applied pressure, which he returned.

A flash of memory made him recall what might have been

that same feeling when he had first met Anne, when they first had that same emotional bonding experience. Did that attraction elicit the same inner conflagration he was now feeling for Sarah? Still, he had spent a lifetime with Anne, more than fifty years. He had fathered her child, stood by her, adjusted to life together. It had been comfortable, respectful, and had engendered a real sense of family.

Anne had been supportive and loyal, the spark plug of his social life and a booster of his ambitions. There were compromises, of course, but that was the essential secret of a long marriage. She had always been more vocal in her prejudices but kept them under control, especially in the complicated communal life of New York.

Of course, he missed her mightily, mourned her deeply, and did not adjust to her absence for a long time after she passed. She had died in the hospital after a massive cerebral hemorrhage that took her as she was recovering from a stroke. He regretted not being present at the moment of her death, but then, he had not been present when his parents had died either.

He and Sarah exchanged glances and smiles as they walked. He had no doubt about her response. Did she feel what he was feeling? Suddenly, Ben stopped and began to sniff the shrubs along the path. They stood quietly as Ben continued his search for whatever had attracted his scent.

Then suddenly, Sarah moved toward Harvey, and they kissed. It was surprisingly long, and their tongues met as well. He felt the faint beginning of tumescence as his body melted into hers, feeling the clear outlines of her bust.

When they parted, he noted that a casual male stroller who had just passed them turned back, looked at them, and smiled. The sight of two very elderly people kissing and embracing in broad daylight must have certainly seemed bizarre. Indeed, he felt strange himself, part of a confusing spectacle. Such activity, he was certain, was not exactly a common occurrence for people in their time of life.

Ben's tug of his leash was the signal for disengagement, and they moved again along the path, still holding hands like young lovers.

"I don't believe this," Sarah said.

"I do," Harvey said, squeezing her hand. "As they say, it's never too late." He deliberately cut the expression short.

"Jesus, Harvey. This is crazy, a silly fantasy."

"It's reality to me, Sarah."

"Not at our age, Harvey. Really."

"Deny it, then," he asserted, as a kind of tease.

She shrugged and giggled as an answer.

They moved toward the exit to the park, holding hands but silent. As the sight of her apartment building loomed closer, he noted again that she looked at her watch.

"You never answered my question, Sarah," Harvey said.

She nodded but remained silent.

"Please, Sarah," he pressed, squeezing her hand. "We mustn't leave this hanging."

"I know, Harvey, but I'm not sure how to cope with this."

"Cope? It seems pretty simple to me."

"It is completely unexpected," Sarah said. "I don't think I know how to handle it."

"Normally, when this kind of a relationship ensues, a key factor is proximity." He chuckled at the formality of his expression. "I'm ready, willing, and able to pursue this, Sarah. Fact is, you now dominate my thoughts and feelings. I want to be with you as much as possible. Simple as that."

They had reached the entrance to her apartment building, and she turned to face him.

"I understand, Harvey. I really do. My reticence has nothing to do with my feelings. I want to be with you. I really do." He noted that her lips were quivering. "I promise you," she grew silent as he saw the signs of struggle in her expression.

"Promise me what?"

"A full explanation."

"I'm not sure I understand what you mean. I never expected this to happen, Sarah. It's a miracle. I...I have feelings, deep feelings for you." He paused and felt a lump grow in his throat. "It's winter for us both, Sarah. You're not supposed to find these things this late." He swallowed hard and took a deep breath.

She stopped walking, faced him, and their eyes locked. Her eyes blurred with tears, and she kissed him again on the lips.

"Give me time," she whispered.

"Sarah, that's the one thing we have in short supply."

"I'm not blind, Harvey. Please. I promise."

"Promise what?"

"An explanation."

She released her hand from his, and the doorman opened the door for her and Shaina. Before she went in, she turned to him.

"Until tomorrow, Harvey. Okay?"

"West Side?"

"West Side."

She turned, entered the lobby, and the door closed behind her. Staring at the closed door, Harvey was baffled and terribly confused. Why the tears? What was the promise all about? It was obvious that she was holding back some terrible secret. He was sure to go through another disturbing night, only this time his anxiety would be tenfold.

He was tempted to enter her apartment building and inquire for her at the desk, demanding an explanation. It was a temptation he resisted, fearing that any inquiry might cause her to sever the relationship or result in a discovery that would be too painful to contemplate.

On the way back across the park, his mind became a welter of suppositions. Perhaps there was a health issue that inhibited their relationship. Sarah had told him she was 75, but that shouldn't matter. He thought of the conversation with George at lunch yesterday when he railed against a cutoff age for seniors and the hint that one day that age would be declared D-Day for everyone.

And here he was, eight years older, living proof that he had won some kind of genetic lottery and was still in reasonable health with all systems functioning well according to his doctor and his own sense of energy and well being. Sarah had declared herself unencumbered by any relationship, and he had believed her. What, then, was the point of her unwillingness to further their friendship?

Did it have anything to do with his not being Jewish? After all, Jews were clannish, wary of non-Jews. Or were they? Hadn't those barriers fallen? Hell, many of his former co-workers were Jewish, and some had become his good friends and colleagues. He amended that thought suddenly, thinking of Anne and her general antipathy to Jews. No, he decided, in this case, it could not apply. They were too old for such things to still matter. For him, he assured himself, it had no relevance. None at all.

He pondered their political differences as a factor, but then, such differences had predated the discovery of their attraction to each other. Hadn't that kiss validated their emotional and physical magnetism? He wondered if this was some kind of a manifestation of senility, some undiagnosed psychological mishap that had forced his mind to imagine that he had regressed to some youthful emotional state.

As he walked, partially dragged by Ben, who stopped occasionally to savor the joys of the autumn-shrouded plants, his meandering thoughts fixated on his own emotional state. By every metric, he could remember from his earliest experiences with the opposite sex, especially with Anne, that he was in love. Why? How did these things happen so fast? Eternal questions with no answers, he sighed. But then, considering his dilemma, when a gift comes your way, snap it up.

He could define his feelings no other way. He was in love, experiencing feelings that had been described since the beginning of recorded time. It was inescapable. He longed for Sarah's presence, the sight of her, her touch. He wanted to hear her voice. He wanted to embrace her, caress her. He felt a sense of joyous intoxication, and the memory of her kiss lingered in his mind as something momentous and unforgettable. Why Sarah? How had it happened? He felt some magical sensation deep in the core of his being.

The realization of what was happening to him brought on a kind of dizziness, and he had to stop at a bench and sit down to restore himself. By the time he had calmed down, a kind of panic began to creep into his thoughts. Without mutuality, he would become a victim of unrequited love, which would be a powerful barrier to the sense of fulfillment his life now required. How could he possibly handle that? Disappointment and rejection at any age were depressing and debilitating.

Time for self-reprimand, he decided, addressing Ben who sat on the ground beside him, occasionally rising when he saw a squirrel.

"Your dad is a stupid old fool," he said. "A man my age acting like some lovesick teenager."

Ben turned to look at his parent.

"Tell me I'm stupid, Ben. Advise me, for crying out loud. Am I being utterly ridiculous?"

Ben looked up, his eyes the picture of absolute unquestioning devotion.

"Some friend you are," he said with a chuckle. He stood up and headed home.

-4-

Sarah arrived at her apartment to find Frank in front of the television set, as usual. Apparently, he had dozed off. His chin rested on his chest but rose when Sarah announced herself. Helena brought out their breakfast and gently awakened her patient. He opened his eyes to sudden confusion. But when he saw Sarah, he smiled and spoke her name. Helena coaxed him to eat, and he did her bidding with some effort.

"How's the old boy?" Sarah said, addressing Frank.

He raised his arm and showed his open palm, which she tapped lightly with her own.

"What are you watching, Frank?"

He looked toward the screen, shrugged, and said nothing.

"Is it a good one?"

He nodded, opening his arms and showing her the palms of his hands.

"Who is in it?" She forced herself to be questioning, anything to spark dialogue. She had looked at the screen and saw the actor Clark Gable.

"Clark?" she said, offering the hint, waiting to see if it registered.

"Clark, Clark, Clark," he repeated.

"Rhymes with table."

"Mable," he said, offering a big smile. "Mable."

"Gable," Sarah said softly, offering a smile.

"Gable, Gable, Gable. Yes, Gable."

"And the lady?" she pressed. Frank looked at the screen, frowning.

"Claudette," she prompted.

"Talbert," he answered tentatively. She exchanged glances with Helena, who observed the interrogation with interest.

"Colbert," she prompted, using the Americanization of the French pronunciation.

"Yes. Yes. Claudette What." Frank looked at her blankly.

She watched him dip his spoon into his oatmeal and, with her help, slowly bring it up to his mouth.

"Remember Venice, Frank? San Paulo Square?"

"Venice?" Frank repeated, frowning, showing no recall. She looked toward Helena, who nodded.

"The violins playing in the background," Sarah pressed. "The sun sparkling in the waters of the Grand Canal. We sat at that little table drinking aperitifs, watching the people. It was like everybody passing by or sitting beside us was in love. We kissed, Frank. Remember that?"

Twenty years ago, she thought. It was glorious. They stayed at the Danieli. She wanted to cry.

"Beautiful Venice," she sighed. "Surely you remember, Frank. We loved Venice, didn't we, Frank?"

She could tell from the blankness in his eyes that he had little recall.

"We took that boat ride to that island. Torcello. Remember? We ate lobsters. It was glorious."

Frank offered a very thin smile, but the blank look in his eyes remained.

"And we got home that day after lobster lunch on the island, and we made love. Then we went up to the roof of the Danieli and had Bellinis and watched the sunset over the lagoon. Venice, Frank. Wonderful Venice."

Sarah observed her husband with sadness. Her eyes moistened, and she turned away. It was increasingly futile. Helena looked at her and shrugged.

The events of the morning had given her a brief sense

of rejuvenation and a rare moment of exhilaration. She likened the kiss to a shot of adrenalin, something that triggered memories of her druggie days, offering the same feeling of the first deep sniff of a line of cocaine. She had felt alive, optimistic, energized, and alert to joyous possibilities. Then, by a kind of association, she had remembered Venice.

"Later we took a gondola."

Frank nodded briefly as if he understood, then his attention flagged.

"You remember that?"

He seemed to nod. Perhaps her memory-jogging had opened up a window in his mind. She nodded toward Helena as if to signal that her prescription for recall might be bearing fruit. Perhaps it was time to press forward. She decided to address his scholarly specialty, Civil War battles. She had tried before to get him engaged but without success, which alarmed her so profoundly that she avoided the subject for weeks.

His brief nod concerning Venice encouraged her to return to the subject in which he was once considered an expert. What she was doing, she realized, was testing the waters in light of what she was experiencing with Harvey, perhaps calculating the speed of Frank's mental descent. Don't go there, she cautioned herself, but she could not resist.

"Pickett's Charge," she said with a glance at Helena who frowned, clearly confused. She had picked one of the best known and bloodiest incidents of the war. Frank nodded and smiled, and she was encouraged.

Frank nodded. "Antietam."

"Frank," she prodded, encouraged. "Gettysburg."

He squinted in confusion. Once he had been an expert on that battle, visiting the battlefield numerous times and lecturing on it for decades. Sometimes his Gettysburg lecture attracted a standing-room-only audience.

She bit her lip and turned to Helena in frustration.

Frank muttered, "Stonewall Jackson."

She could not go on and turned her face away to wipe the tears that had, without warning, rolled down her cheeks.

"Lee's horse's name was Traveller," Frank mumbled suddenly. Sarah nodded, filled now with terror and guilt. Actually, he had gotten that right. But where had such a thought come from?

"White," Frank muttered, smiling thinly, his expression childlike.

"Yes, it was," Sarah said, clearing her throat. "And quite beautiful."

Frank nodded. Then his brief alertness flagged. It was time to change the subject.

"Have you had a good morning so far?" Sarah asked, forcing a smile, patting his upper arm and then taking his hand and kissing it.

He nodded, his eyes drifting back to the television screen. "I'm glad."

Sarah looked toward Helena, who nodded in approval and said, "Yes, we had a good morning, didn't we, Mr. Silverman?"

Frank nodded.

"And how was your morning, Mrs. Silverman?" Helena asked, prompting her as she often did to keep the conversation going.

"Very good." Sarah knew the dialogue by rote, reduced to a series of empty phrases. She wished she could tell them what a really lovely morning it had been, how she had been with this man, how she had enjoyed the experience. To Helena, she knew it would sound like a betrayal.

Now, watching her debilitated childlike husband, she felt like she was drowning in guilt and despair. Despite her attempts to interest him in their past life together, despite her caring, despite her sacrifice and devotion, it was more and more obvious that her husband was coming closer to the brink of the dark hole of totally cancelled memory. Worse, she found herself calculating the speed of his decline, knowing exactly what had put that thought into her mind.

Helena, although difficult, demanding, and often arrogant, was doing her job, advocating solely for the patient, forcing Sarah to do her duty and make the passage to oblivion of her charge as smooth as possible. Of course, Helena had predicted the course of Frank's disease at their initial interview after she had carefully observed and met her future patient. She had assessed the situation and articulated what she believed was happening to him in her singsong accented but very precise English.

"Your husband will very soon need full-time, around-the-clock care. His dementia will increase, and, of course, his various physical ailments will also have a debilitating effect. You told me that you have promised yourself never to put him into an institution. Is this true?"

"Absolutely," Sarah had answered with militant affirmation at that first interview. "I would never, never break that promise. We made a solemn pledge to each other when it became apparent that Frank was beginning to fail. He understood then what was going to happen to him. I swore I would never let him leave his home and be left to die among strangers. I will keep my word."

Hadn't he saved her, resurrected her life? She owed him that. Integrity and compassion were the ideals she valued above all. It was the foundation of her views, the heart of her liberalism, her feeling for the plight of the other, the less fortunate, the downtrodden. In her imagination, she heard her daughter Sheila applaud.

Frank had embodied that philosophy as well. Without such feelings of commonality, she believed implicitly there could be no progress and that the endgame for progress was equality, sharing, benevolence, justice, and, above all, self sacrifice and a genuine feeling for the plight of the less fortunate. That was her bedrock principle and the very heart of her motivation. It was the sustaining idea of her life.

Her mantra was that one must be loyal to one's ideals, not only in one's political conduct but in one's personal life. There could be no compromise. To Sarah, self-sacrifice, especially as it impacted her promise to Frank, was the true test of her integrity. Wasn't it?

One of the caveats of Helena's employment was that Sarah strictly adhere to a code of conduct that fit well with her own ministrations to her husband. Helena had explained that a person with close ties to an afflicted patient, especially a life partner in a long-term relationship, could be of enormous assistance to someone entering into a state of dementia and that the comfort of a loved one's presence could help delay a complete shutdown of awareness. Sarah agreed wholeheartedly to the commitment and so far had followed it to the letter.

Helena, with her God-given vision, proved authoritative and assertive. She obliged Sarah with a running commentary of expectations, all attributed to some master plan ordained by God. Although Sarah paid lip service to the spiritual nature of her comments, she did believe in the fidelity of Helena's medical information regarding the progression of Frank's disease.

"I have experienced patients at all stages of dementia," Helena told her. "Treating physical illnesses has very traditional protocols, but when it comes to dementia, it is far more unpredictable. There are moments of clarity, but they diminish with time. Behavior becomes an issue. There is paranoia and anger that must be dealt with, and sometimes violence. And worse. They will be doubly incontinent, unable to control themselves. They will not know how to dress themselves. They will be unable to write, and many will be unable to talk. They will not recognize who you are. If you are truly sincere about your commitment to your husband to be involved in his caretaking and to keep him at home, you must trust my judgment, Mrs. Silverman."

That meant, as she explained, strict scheduling with as little deviation from the established routine as possible. Deviations very often upset patients, she pointed out, and made her work more difficult. Sarah sensed there was an element of threat in her remarks, and up until then, she had been very careful not to cross the line and incur her wrath. But even worse, her leaving would be a disaster. Without her, she would be bereft.

"I really insist that you must cooperate," Helena told Sarah right at the beginning. And Sarah, actually ecstatic at finding someone so committed and efficient, had agreed and so far complied almost to the letter. When Sarah explained that she was interested in preserving her own health to be in shape to assist Frank and outlined her yoga schedule, Helena had, of course, agreed. She also told Helena that she would like to find time to pursue her various political and social causes, to which Helena was not as sanguine.

"I am needed," Sarah pointed out. "I just can't abandon them."

"I'm afraid you will have to become less involved as time goes on."

"Less involved?"

"As long as the patient's needs come first. Keeping your husband at home is a challenge. God needs us to carry out his mission. You've made your choice, Mrs. Silverman. And I'm here to help you fulfill that choice. Your husband is incurable, and his decline can go on for years."

"Years?"

"There is a timeline, but even God knows it is not precise. The final stage is the most challenging."

"I understand, Helena." Actually, through her own research, Sarah had learned that a spouse who chooses to be a sole caretaker might actually falter first due to the tension and aggravation involved in the process. Some even become as mentally challenged as the patient. It was scary.

Helena had explained that mornings were especially important for a patient with this kind of a condition since it was the time of most clarity. Hence her insistence that Sarah and Frank have breakfast together and that Sarah spend as much time as possible in his proximity. Nights and weekends were presented as additional difficulties.

So far, Sarah had managed the nights since Frank was not too erratic of a sleeper and not a wanderer, which often afflicted dementia patients. Lately, there had been some disturbances, a screaming nightmare, incontinence, paranoia. Sarah dealt with them, knowing that at some point she would have to hire Helena full-time, night and day, which would constitute a potentially killing expense.

Shaina, their aging poodle, was an asset, Helena pointed out. Dementia patients were comfortable with pets, and Sarah was determined to keep her. The poodle had a calming effect on Frank, who had been her principal overseer. He adored her. Now, walking Shaina and maintaining her, which once was Frank's delight, fell completely on Sarah's shoulders. Rather than a chore, it turned out to be a godsend, getting Sarah out of the apartment in the morning and a number of times during the day. But her meeting with Harvey had suddenly presented an unwanted complication.

It had come about quite by accident, and its strange circumstances became a repetitive topic in her mind. She had walked to the East Side lawn because she had needed to clear her head from a particularly trying night with Frank. The walk to the East Side was reviving and the conversation with Harvey unusual since she normally did not socialize with any of her fellow dog parents.

Recalling the coincidence, she marveled at the engagement and the underlying hostility of their initial conversation. A serious relationship with a man, despite an occasional sexual fantasy, was far, far out of her radar range. Age and her present circumstances were powerful inhibitors. From every logical perspective, that part of her life was over, certainly for now, perhaps forever.

Such things do not happen to people in their 80s, she had insisted to herself when this strange feeling came over her. Love at her age and Harvey's was some kind of a joke. And the kiss? It was as if she were seized by a kind of fever.

She was never a devotee of romance novels or other media renditions of romantic love, and her youthful experiences had taught her the fragility of believing in the permanence of such feelings. Even her initial attraction to Frank, although powerful in its own way, did not reach the explosive hold on her emotions that had suddenly now assailed her. She felt in the grip of something that seemed uncommonly compelling, and at first, she dismissed it as ridiculous and imaginary. The kiss changed that original analysis, although the illogic of it remained.

She was aware as well that her reticence to connect further with Harvey was hurtful and confusing to him. Troubling her, too, was the lie she had told him.

She had lied about her age and her married state, hoping it would make her seem more enticing and available. Even that idea was an anomaly since she was thinking more like a woman half her age, at least. She had actually made herself appear as available. She had led him on.

Harvey had boasted about his 83 years, which he acknowledged as a sort of miracle milestone, showing off the fact that his condition belied his number. Still, she had reacted to his attention, catching and returning the signals.

Then there was the Jewish question. Scratch a goy and underneath lurked an anti-Semite. Now that was over the top, she admonished herself, disgusted by her own clichéd intolerance. He hadn't given her the slightest indication of such prejudice.

She knew, despite all the imagined obstacles churning in her mind, that she was resolving the issue realistically. Where was the harm? Indeed, didn't she deserve such a respite from the crushing burden of her situation?

In fact, as she surveyed the sad wreckage of what had constituted her married life, watching her infirm husband disintegrate, she saw herself, as if for the first time, as a victim, a designation that she had fought against since her husband was first diagnosed with his various illnesses, especially the onset of dementia or Alzheimer's, an often blurred diagnosis. What had started out as martyrdom was morphing into victimization, a dangerous idea that could undermine her solemn pledge to Frank.

She spent the day in a quandary, vacillating from acceptance to rejection, meaning that either she would yield to this strangely evocative feeling and pursue the relationship with Harvey or reject the idea and make an effort to push any thoughts of him and the possibilities from her mind. Logic told her to resist. But there was something else at work on her psyche that had little to do with logic and seemed to have a life of its own.

In obedience to a bizarre protocol, she stripped and viewed her naked body in the full-length mirror in the bathroom, assessing herself with a lot of detail. If there was an impending relationship, she suspected and actually hoped it would include a caress of the flesh or some version of it. A platonic relationship, she reasoned, would not be worth the candle. She needed a lot more than a mere friend. The kiss and its reaction had taught her that.

Considering her conflicting position in connection with Harvey, she was surprised at such sexual meandering. Still, she could not deny the fact that he had aroused her feelings. Was this love, whatever love was? Again and again she marveled at the idea of it, the sense of need that it engendered, the longing it inspired.

Before she drew away from the mirror, she inspected her face. Her skin had wrinkled beside her eyes, and a jowly droopiness had set in beside her jaws. Her teeth, which had some scattered transplants, were white enough to enhance her smile, and her blue nugget eyes were, like her breasts, her most attractive feature that seemed to retain their luster, or so she hoped.

She lifted her hands and pushed them through her tight grey curls. They were once as black as charcoal with eyebrows to match, equally grey now. Years ago when the grey first arrived, she had colored her hair to its original color. But she had long abandoned the practice. Perhaps she would do it again, she thought.

When this exercise in vanity was finally over, she felt suddenly as if she had regressed to her little girl self when she had applied her mother's lipstick and powdered her face and dressed in her clothes, including her high-heeled shoes, and stood in front of a three-way mirror.

She clearly remembered the image of herself, posing in various attitudes she had seen in fashion magazines and feeling the incipient joys of oncoming womanhood. Remembering, she doubled up in a fit of hysterical laughter. Am I going bonkers?

It struck her that through all this sturm and drang, she had not considered what Harvey was feeling. Was it similar in scope to what she was feeling? He had actually declared himself, but what did such a declaration mean to an older man? Was he going through the same agonizing appraisal of what he was feeling? Was he longing for her embrace, having sexual thoughts, thinking about her, unable to get her out of his mind? Stupid old man, she whispered aloud. How dare you disrupt my life? You have your gall, you fucking right-wing goy. Then she whispered her apology. Sorry, baby. Shut up and kiss me again.

Of course, he was unencumbered, single, certainly lonely, or at the least alone. She had dismissed the idea that he, too, was telling lies, but then a man in search of an affair was not immune to constructing a false façade to gain his ends. If only that were true, she thought, amused by the idea. She rejected the premise in his case.

Was it merely the company of a woman he sought? Or something more complex, more overwhelming? Was he having sexual thoughts about her? Good God, she thought. Where is this going?

Give it time, she decided finally as she watched Frank look at the television screen. Clark and Claudette were still acting out the fantasy of the movie. Suddenly, as if he had sensed her, he looked at her and smiled and then held out his hand to hers and squeezed it. Obviously, he still recognized her presence and was comforted by it. She forced herself to tamp down a rising sob.

Throughout the day, she continued to agonize over what was now a should-I-or-shouldn't-I dilemma. She went through her normal chores in a haze, walking Shaina, browsing through the news on her computer, ordering Fresh Direct groceries, and debating with herself to the point of mental exhaustion.

Frank continued to watch the television screen throughout the day. He was quiet and, as usual, carefully monitored by Helena who helped prepare a light dinner and dress him for bed.

By morning, after what was a comparatively quiet night, Sarah was still undecided about how she was going to react to this new complication in her life. At one point, she decided to avoid the West Side dog area entirely until she remembered that Harvey knew where she lived, and if he was as involved with her as he had indicated, he was surely going to attempt to visit her.

It was still dark when Sarah leashed a somewhat confused Shaina, and, instead of proceeding to the West Side dog area, swiftly walked along the park paths to the East Side, checking her watch, as if she had to beat the clock. She reached the East Side opening, which brought her to Fifth Avenue and 66th Street, where she knew Number One Fifth was located, just across from the park entrance.

The sun was just peeking above the eastern high-rises as she stood in expectation, waiting for Harvey and Ben to come marching across the street. Traffic along Fifth was still somewhat thin, and from where she stationed herself, she could see the entrance to his apartment building. Her assumption was that he would soon exit the building and head to the park.

She acknowledged that what she was doing was a weird reaction to her dilemma, and she still had no fixed idea of what course of action she was going to pursue, only that she and he had better talk things out. She had no idea of the *what* and *why* of it and was totally confused by her conduct. Yet she continued to wait impatiently for him and Ben to show themselves. She continued to glance nervously at her watch.

Then it occurred to her that she might as well enter the apartment building and ask someone to ring him, an idea that she quickly rejected. Suppose he had lied and there was a wife or significant other with whom he shared the apartment. Her embarrassment would be acute, and she would be humiliated for falling for such a brazen lie.

Before she could act, she saw Harvey and Ben. They were standing on the curb waiting for the Fifth Avenue light to change. He had not seen her. There was still time to retreat, go back to the West Side. Would he think she was pursuing him? No, she told herself. We are here to discuss the situation. Nothing more.

But then Shaina barked and pulled on her leash, and it was too late to make any other decision. Sarah felt both elated and trapped. Suddenly, Harvey was in front of her, and they were embracing. Again, they kissed, deeper this time than yesterday.

"I'm stunned," Harvey said when they had disengaged.

"I can imagine," Sarah said before they kissed again.

"I had a terrible night," Harvey said. Holding hands, they moved into the park. Sharp beams of sunlight had begun to reveal the trees and the partly withered fall leaves that had not yet descended.

"East or west?" Harvey asked. Sarah shrugged, smiled, turned toward him, and they kissed again.

"West," Sarah said. Despite her action, she was still committed to be back at her usual hour. Oddly, she had not thought about that commitment until that moment.

They moved slowly, stopping only when the dogs began their sniffing routines.

Suddenly, Sarah moved to a nearby bench, bringing Harvey along, and they sat down. Harvey looked at her, obviously confused, and for awhile she sat silently, pondering how to begin.

"I lied, Harvey," Sarah began, her voice breaking. She held tightly to his hand, squeezing it. "I'm married."

Harvey's complexion paled.

"But," she continued, holding a finger over his mouth, "my husband is very ill, under nursing care during the day. On top of his physical ailments, he has dementia. Alzheimer's, his doctors say. I am committed to keeping him at home no matter how he declines." She squeezed his hand. "Harvey, darling. I hate that I lied to you, but that's the emmis."

"Emmis?"

"Yiddish slang for the truth."

He smiled, nodded, and they kissed again.

"I just wanted to clear the air," she whispered.

"I knew there had to be a good reason for your reluctance."

"That's not all, Harvey."

"You mean there's more emmis?" He appeared suddenly apprehensive.

"I'm not 75, darling. I'm 80."

"Really?" Harvey said, feigning surprise. "You don't look a day over 60."

"Now who's lying? Are you really a widower, Harvey?"

Their eyes locked. He chuckled.

"There is a moratorium on lying when you hit the 80s. It is now official that we have both passed the rubicon where all falsehood does not exist. Yes, I am a widower, and yes, I am really 83."

She was silent for a long moment.

"There's more, Harvey."

"More emmis?"

She nodded.

"I have to adhere to a strict schedule ordered by my husband's caretaker. I must be back," she looked at her watch, "in time to share breakfast with my husband. I must obey his caretaker's orders to the letter or I will lose her. Everything I do must conform to her schedule in caring for Frank, that's my husband. I owe him my life, Harvey. We have been married 50 years. I will never, never allow him to die among strangers."

She paused, and they just looked at each other.

"In other words, I am caught between a rock and a hard place. I want to be with you, I really do, darling. Something has happened deep inside me. I don't know why or how. It's crazy, I know."

"Very," he agreed.

"I'm sorry, Harvey."

"Nothing to be sorry for. We should be celebrating."

"You have moved me, Harvey. Very much."

"And vice versa."

"It could be a kind of phase."

"Maybe."

"A geriatric silliness."

"Maybe so," said Harvey, "but I don't want it to go away. I want to be with you."

She sighed and grew thoughtful.

"We could be kidding ourselves," she shrugged.

"We'll find out, then," Harvey said. "But I don't want it to end."

"Nor do I."

"Surely there must be a way," Harvey added.

"We still have the mornings," she said, offering a broad smile. She looked at the dogs. "Them." She squeezed his hand.

"True, but." She put a finger to his lips. "I have been thinking about it, wracking my brain," Harvey went on.

She laughed. "You know what we are, Harvey?

He looked at her, squinting, puzzled.

"Two alter kocker meshuganas."

"Whatever that means."

"Two crazy old people playing with fantasy."

"In love," Harvey said, kissing her again.

"Maybe," she said, shaking her head, and they kissed again.

"No maybes, Sarah."

They locked gazes, and she felt the power of their mutual feelings.

"The problem, Harvey, is logistics."

"Logistics?" He was clearly confused.

She explained the situation from her perspective, reminding him of the so-called rules of engagement set down by Helena.

"Everything is set in stone, Harvey. Helena is a martinet.

I need her badly. If I rouse her ire, I don't know how I'll cope, and I won't under any circumstances put Frank in an institution. I won't be able to live with myself." She looked at Harvey. "Hence, the rules of engagement." She looked at her watch. "You see, there will always be the pull of the rules. Until, and I'm not going to go there, Harvey."

Harvey nodded.

"I think I understand." He seemed tentative. "Are we then doomed to meet in the early mornings at the dog runs?"

She shook her head.

"I'm not a complete prisoner, darling. There are still windows of time Helena agreed to. I do yoga a couple times a week, and I told her I still have meetings."

"And at night?"

"Night?"

"Go out for dinner. Be together. Mostly that. Be together. Maybe cuddle."

She looked upward and laughed. "Cuddle? You're kidding."

"Maybe more," he said with trepidation.

"Sounds like a proposition," she said, winking.

"Anything is possible," he whispered.

"You're talking affair, you know."

Harvey was silent for a long moment. "A clandestine affair."

She let the idea simmer for a long moment. It had a promising connotation. She did not pursue it. Instead, she moved closer to him, and they kissed again, deeply, tongues intertwined.

Then she lifted her hand and looked at her watch. "Oh my God," she said, rising from the bench. "I'm late." She stood up, and they walked together at her swift pace, which mirrored her anxiety. The dogs struggled to keep up, stopping often to obey their sniffing sensations and satisfy nature's needs.

At the park exit on Central Park West, they halted and kissed again. By then she had decided on a plan.

"This afternoon at three," she said, "at your apartment."

"You'll be there?" he frowned, as if doubtful.

"Of course, I'll be there. I promise."

"I don't know what to say."

"Hold it until three. We'll talk." She met his gaze and winked.

"I'll be waiting."

She had planned to attend her yoga class in the afternoon twice a week. She would skip that. She was part of a voluntary people's committee dealing with drafting recommendations about more compassionate policing that met once a week in the afternoon. The chairman was aware of her problems and would not question her absence, however frequent. With clever scheduling she would make time to be with Harvey.

The excitement of the morning with Harvey stimulated by the fervor of their embraces had given the arrangement new impetus. He was right, of course. It was indeed fated to be a clandestine affair, largely because of the boundaries of her other demands. The phrase itself—clandestine affair—offered the undeniable promise of sexual activity. Still, she knew her anticipation might be inflated by her own needs. She decided that she owed it to herself to test the waters.

They exchanged cell phone numbers, each immediately labeling them with a name. This relationship was, for her, a symbol of freedom, a tempting respite from the hard burdens of her obligation to Frank. It suggested rebellion, triggering memories of youthful protest, defiance, anarchy, and renewal. She pushed such memories away, mustering resistance. That era had long passed. Her priority was Frank. His needs came first. She must live to the letter of her promise. Case closed.

As for what she was currently experiencing, think of it as

a daring experiment, she speculated, searching for some rational explanation. Recreation. Amusement. Naughty mischief. As for *love*, she let the word bounce in her mind like a silver ball in a pinball machine, making musical sounds, fun to watch. Why not? A few pulls won't hurt.

He walked her to the entrance of her apartment. The anticipation of their afternoon meeting offered a shivering sense of transport, a physical sensation that she needed to corral and discipline. As they exchanged glances at parting, after yet another embrace, she felt her heartbeat accelerate.

"I'll be waiting, darling," Harvey said, kissing her hand before releasing it. As he did so, she noted the curiosity of the doorman. She felt a brief tremor of guilt. She acknowledged his greeting with a smile and a nod and proceeded to the elevators.

-5-

The reality of their upcoming tryst became clear to Harvey the moment he entered his own apartment. A wave of panic swept over him, and its first manifestation was the condition of his apartment. He quickly set about cleaning it, gathering piles of newspapers and the three-day accumulation of kitchen garbage, the usual hazardous waste of the bachelor life. He dispatched the detritus down the chute in the trash room.

A maid came in once a week but was not due until tomorrow. He wondered about hospitality in the middle of the afternoon. Perhaps wine, some hors d'oeuvres, tea or coffee, and cake. He had never entertained a woman alone in his apartment. In encounters with the opposite sex during the earlier days of his widowerhood, he would be entertained in the woman's apartment, not his own. Anne would have known how to handle it. The irony of the thought was troubling.

His apartment building had its own dining room and offered room service as well, but he discovered that three in the afternoon was not the best time for kitchen service, and he decided to prepare something on his own.

He rushed down to the liquor store and bought some bottles of Dom Pérignon at the cost of $300 per bottle. Was he overdoing it? This was a celebration, wasn't it? The store offered frozen hors d'oeuvres, and he bought a few packages to stock up in anticipation of other visits.

His excitement and nervousness were intense. He arranged Anne's beloved Chinese imported china on the cocktail table in front of the couch, unwrapped the frozen hors d'oeuvres and arranged them artistically on a large decorative plate, hoping they would thaw out by three. He put the Champagne in the fridge and found their old ice bucket and stand in the hall closet and put them next to the cocktail table.

Then he half-shuttered the blinds in the living room, leaving just enough space to catch the rays of the declining sun. He was, after all, not immune to his own vanity and Sarah's as well. The aging body did not look well in harsh light.

By 2:00, he had the apartment ready to receive Sarah. By then, wild anticipation had turned into abject fear. What was expected of him? A few years before, after an unsuccessful and humiliating episode with a woman, he had consulted his doctor who had prescribed Viagra, which seemed to solve the problem, but he had never taken the test with a live female, mostly out of fear of non-performance.

It was he, in his excitement, who had dubbed their assignation a clandestine affair. The designation clearly meant that a sexual episode was expected. He was certain that she understood its meaning and might be fully prepared to participate. Or not. Whatever her expectation, he supposed he had better be open to the possibility. His insecurity was palpable.

He rummaged in his bathroom medicine chest hoping to find the old Viagra pills, and when they couldn't be found, he inspected every drawer in the apartment. Perhaps he threw them away. He was panicked. And if he did find them, would they have retained their potency?

Finally, as the hours progressed, he gave up the search for the pills. How would she react if he couldn't perform the primal act of copulation?

He imagined her reaction to his failure to rise to the occasion. She would soothe him, of course, and show sensitivity and understanding, the ultimate cliché of the disappointed woman. Would he have to explain that he couldn't find the

Viagra? Good God, he thought, what could be more humiliating than that? Worse, he had learned from his rare solo episodes that even without an erection, he could have an orgasm, a disastrous outcome in this situation.

He felt a cold sweat pop out on his back, moistening his shirt, which reminded him that he had better shower, which he did. He brushed his teeth twice and rinsed his mouth with Listerine. He rolled on his deodorant and then shaved again and swathed his face with scented aftershave.

Then he changed into khakis, slipped on loafers without socks, and put on a sports shirt with the three top buttons left unfastened. He imagined he was dressed to look macho with curly gray hairs showing on his chest. Even that seemed so retro. In fact, everything anticipatory seemed retro.

Appraising himself in the full-length mirror, he was discouraged. He did not look the part of an eager lover and knew in his gut that what he was offering was more blab than jab. As an ex-advertising man, he knew he had over-promised the qualities of his so-called product. But he could not deny his feelings for Sarah. That part, he assured himself, was genuine. So was the general appearance of his aging body, despite the compliments about not looking his age and the smooching they had done in the park. Who was he kidding?

He berated himself. He had given her a false picture. His pretense to youthfulness was a sham. He was frightened. Pulling out his cell phone, he searched for her number. He would call her and cancel their so-called clandestine assignation. No, he decided. She might as well discover the truth. He was nothing more than an old phony, a liar, a fantasizer.

While he waited, he paced the apartment, remembering their embraces and kisses, remembering, too, that he had felt the beginning of tumescence. He imagined her breasts, the image of which seemed to help somewhat. By the time

3:00 rolled around, he was a nervous wreck.

She was prompt to the minute. The man at the lobby desk announced her, and Harvey asked him to send her up. His palms began to sweat. He felt all thumbs, socially inept, unprepared, frightened. But when he opened the door for her, they embraced and he kissed her hard on the mouth, their tongues caressing, his tension beginning to dissipate. From the scent of her, he knew she had prepared herself. He felt butterflies in his stomach.

At the sound of the door buzzer, Ben had stirred, dancing around the embracing couple. "Sorry kid, your lady friend was otherwise engaged," she said, after they had separated, patting his head and kissing his snout. She wore a brown cloth jacket over a pleated brown skirt. Harvey took her jacket, and underneath was a tight, azure blue sweater that emphasized her ample bust and matched the color of her eyes. Her short curly hair was gorgeously white, and the color of her eyes was embellished by the sun's rays that peeked through the slits of the blinds. In this muted light, she looked remarkably youthful.

The feel of her breasts in their close embrace helped quell his earlier fears, although it did not completely dissipate them. Releasing her, he noted that she carefully inspected the apartment, roaming around the living room, stopping to observe the many plaques and awards he had won during his career.

"I'm impressed, Harvey," she said, reaching out to hold his hand. "Quite an array." He wanted to make his usual joke about being an expert in seducing people to part with their money but hesitated for fear of setting off a political firestorm. They embraced again, and this time, he could not resist putting a hand on her breast and squeezing.

"Nature's gift," she giggled. "I brought them along for your pleasure."

He searched his mind for a comeback line, but his anxiety blocked his thoughts. Instead, he kissed her again, held her, lingered, then disengaged. She moved to the couch and crossed her legs. He pulled the bottle out of the ice bucket and popped the cork.

"Well, well," she said with a seductive wink. "All the trimmings. Wow! Dom Pérignon." She reached for an hors d'oeuvre, popped it in her mouth, and then spit it out.

"Still frozen, Harvey," she said, laughing.

"I'm all thumbs, Sarah," he admitted. "Nervous as hell."

"Believe me, Harvey, you're not alone," she said, smiling. She reached for the Champagne flute and held it out to be filled. He noted as he poured that his hand shook. Then he poured his own and sat beside her, and they clinked glasses.

"To my gorgeous West Side sweetheart," he said.

"L' Chaim."

"I know that one, Sarah. L'Chaim." He drank deeply. "What does it mean?"

"To life," she said. "Didn't you goys see *Fiddler on the Roof*?"

Of course. He had seen it with Anne, who had whispered in his ear as everyone gave the cast a standing ovation, "They are all still peasants." Nevertheless, she had admitted to enjoying the performance.

"I thought it was quite wonderful," he told her, hoping she would not think him overly solicitous. It did not seem to faze her. They held hands, and he brought one up to his lips and kissed her palm.

When he moved to look at her face, he noted that her lips were trembling and her eyes were moist.

"Tears?" he whispered, reaching for a paper napkin and wiping them away.

"You can't imagine, Harvey." She could not go on, and rather than talk, she finished her Champagne in one long draught. He emptied his glass as well. She offered hers again, and he filled it as well as his own, raising it in another toast. "L'Chaim," he said. "Yes. To life. That is exactly the point. To be alive is everything."

She paused, looking as if her thoughts were drifting. "Not quite everything, Harvey. To be alive and aware is everything."

"I'll buy that," Harvey said, sensing her meaning.

"L'Chaim," she said again. "Let's live it as if it were the first day of our lives."

"L'Chaim," he repeated. They clinked again and drank deeply.

"Takes the edge off," she sighed after a deep swallow.

"I hope so."

They upended their glasses and placed them on the cocktail table. He bent over and kissed her, placing a hand on her breast. The feel of it both excited and calmed him, but desire did not offer any tangible evidence where it counted. She nodded and caressed his face.

"I thank God for this, Harvey." Then she shook her head vigorously. "No," she said, obviously reacting to some inner dialogue. "I will not begin this with the long sad story." She hesitated, reached over for another napkin, wiped her teary eyes, and blew her nose.

"This calls for cheers, not tears," Harvey said. He was unsure about how to react. He hadn't expected her to cry.

"I did not intend to spoil the moment, Harvey."

"You haven't spoiled anything," he said, "I can't believe my luck."

"Our luck, Harvey. Our nachas."

"Nachas?"

She shrugged and, having recovered, giggled nervously. "Do I have to translate?"

"Not this time. I get the sense of it."

He drew her closer, squeezed her breast, and kissed her deeply and long.

"Actually, it's been a long time since I felt anything like this, Harvey."

"You're not alone, Sarah."

"It's all very mysterious, boobala."

"Boobala?"

"A Yiddish word of endearment. Darling."

He chuckled.

"Endear away."

She kissed his ear and placed a hand on his thigh. He felt a brief panic, which quickly subsided. He was reacting.

"I'm not going to overanalyze it. But this I must say: I have all the symptoms of a man in love."

"I certainly hope so, Harvey," she said coquettishly. They kissed, and he again squeezed her breast.

"I can't stop thinking about you, Sarah. And I long for you in a way that I can barely understand. Considering my age."

"No." She put her finger on his lips. "Lots of ways to look at it, Harvey. Let's not get hung up with numbers. Better to deal with an established concern than a novice."

"I hope I can measure up to that assessment," he said, chuckling, feeling the Champagne buzz begin to kick in.

Suddenly, to his consternation, she looked at her watch. She caught a glimpse of his disapproval.

"Habit, darling. Sorry. We are in yoga class."

"How much time do we really have, Sarah?" He corrected himself quickly. It was, of course, the crux of the matter. He quickly self-corrected to a fallback position. "I mean, this afternoon."

"Couple of hours," she whispered. "And I can get a cab."

He forced a chuckle, understanding the meaning of her explanation, alert to the necessity to avoid the subject. He reached over and poured them a refill, emptying the bottle.

"You mustn't get me drunk," she said as they watched each other take a deep sip from their glasses. "I might do something naughty."

He was too frightened to respond, but he was feeling the first real signs of tumescence.

They kissed deeply again, and this time he put his hand on her flesh beneath her sweater and squeezed her breasts.

"I've been fantasizing about these," he whispered.

"They're not what they used to be, Harvey. "

"What is?"

Without comment, she sat up, lifted her sweater and removed her brassiere. In the muted light, she lifted her breasts and moved closer to him. He reached out and caressed them.

"They're beautiful," he said, caressing them, tonguing a nipple.

He felt a blood surge in his cock as he kneaded the soft mounds.

"I've dreamt about this, Sarah."

"So have I. They've been sadly neglected, darling. Until now."

"Should we go into the bedroom, sweetheart?" Harvey whispered. The question surprised him. Insecurity still dogged him.

She shook her head.

"Let's live it like a real seduction, Harvey. I like the idea, how did you put it? Clandestine? Secret? Compulsive? Sexy? Our secret?" She caressed his crotch. "Let's stay on the couch. It's a great prop for a seduction and," she giggled, "I came here to be violated."

"I love these, Sarah. Love them." He put his head between her breasts, encouraged.

"Call them tits, Harvey. Let's use the real words and not mess with propriety."

She reached for his crotch, feeling its length beneath his pants. They caressed each other for some time. He was surprised how quickly it was happening.

"We found an oasis in the desert, Harvey," she said as

if reading his mind.

Suddenly, she looked up.

"I love this, Harvey." Her tongue moistly caressed the length of his cock as she caressed his balls. He felt the blood surge.

"Tell you the truth, I was worried."

"In my experienced judgment, darling, your goyish shmeckel is in reasonably good working order."

He felt his erection growing under her ministrations. His anxiety was dissipating, and he began to feel the onset of pleasure. What worried him now was that he would either come too fast or lose his erection. He brought his hand down to inspect it. Not rock hard, but adequate for insertion, he decided, optimistically.

"I hope it holds," he said.

She came alive under his touch and began to move her hips against him, manipulating him again, moving down again, bringing him to another passable erection. He moved his hand to his prick. Not like hard steel, but serviceable, he thought.

"This is it, baby," she cried. Her breath came in gasps. He was astonished.

"I can't believe this," he said after they had cooled. "I feel like a kid who just passed a test."

"With a fairly good grade," she giggled.

A thin film of perspiration had formed on his back. They stayed locked together for some time, and then she stirred, raised herself.

"I had my doubts," he admitted.

"I didn't," she whispered.

"I couldn't find the Viagra," he confessed, laughing.

She balanced herself on her elbow and studied his face.

"I got here a bull man," she said, raising her voice and offering mock applause. "Can you imagine if you found the pills?" She shrugged and grew thoughtful. "I pondered the possibility, Harvey. I admit it. Frankly, I expected you might need some help. You've overwhelmed my expectations, even *au naturel*. Let's call it a bonus."

"And if it didn't happen?"

"Oy, that sounds so Jewish. It happened, Harvey. Remember, we fell in love without the sex. Just being in your arms would have been satisfaction enough." She shrugged. "Maybe a little white lie," she sighed. "I hoped for this other dimension, Harvey. I would have tried my damndest." She stopped abruptly. "It's a hard image for me to dump, Harvey."

"For you?"

"Just tell me where to draw the line, darling. "

He grew thoughtful. "I never did this with a Jewish girl," he said.

"I guess you just got lucky," she giggled.

"Are all Jewish girls like this?" he mused, kissing her breasts.

"I never did a survey. There are a lot of jokes about this. Mostly negative." She shrugged. "I've always been a red hot madel." She paused. "Girl." Then she giggled again."Will true confessions turn you on, boobala? I got lots of stories to tell about my wild youth in the sack. I guess I was ahead of my time. I was a bit of a coorva."

"Coorva?"

"Whore. Well, not indiscriminate in that sense." Her body suddenly shook with laughter. "I guess I was named Sarah for a subliminal reason."

"How so?"

"As the biblical story goes, Abraham and his wife Sarah were crossing into Egypt. Sarah was a beauty, and when the Pharaoh got word that she was a knockout, he wanted her for himself. Abraham, no dummy when it came to survival skills, identified her as his sister instead of his wife, which probably saved his life since the Pharaoh would have ordered his execution. Thus Sarah spent some time sexually administering to the Pharaoh. One supposes she did a helluva job, and eventually the Pharaoh let her go."

"If she was such a hot number, why let her go?"

She tickled his ribs. "Maybe he wanted to save some for the rest of his harem."

They discovered how much they loved finding humor in everything, the joyfulness of abandon. He noted, too, how she loved laughter and how it made her seem younger. He discovered in their playfulness a kind of resurrection of youthfulness.

"I was named after a six-foot rabbit," Harvey said, adding to the silliness. Actually, he was born before the rabbit was created, and he was actually named after his grandfather, an austere pharmacist.

"I saw the play and the movie," she said. "Actually, it's a rather stupid name."

"I wasn't consulted," Harvey said, extending their laughter.

"If somebody would have told me I would be doing this in my 80s, I would have laughed them out of the park."

"You're not alone."

"Let's squeeze the grapefruit for the last drop."

He turned to embrace her, and they kissed as he kneaded her breasts.

There was a long silence in which he pondered his past. "My Anne could have done without it," he mused.

"I'm sorry," she said.

"And your husband?"

"In his prime, he was quite wonderful," she said, after a long pause. "It seems so long ago." She turned toward him. "It's pretty awful, Harvey. The way he is. He's barely continent."

"I love being here with you, Sarah. You and I." He patted her cheek. "I love you, Sarah. I never thought."

"Me, too, Harvey."

"I want you to share your life with me, darling. I want that more than anything. Bottom line for me, Sarah. Us together always. Day and night. Night and day. Never alone."

"I wish, Harvey, but let's leave the bottom-line discussion for another day."

"At our age, Sarah, there is only one line—the finish line." He surprised himself by his emphatic and philosophical tone, reminding him of his friend George. "We've defied the odds, darling. Let's accept the gift."

"Haven't I?"

"Partially."

"Let's not go there, darling. I'm committed."

"But if we love each other?"

She put a finger over his lips. "Don't spoil it, Harvey. Please. Promise me. Leave it alone. Not now. It's not up for discussion."

"When, then?"

"Please, Harvey. There is no when."

"However you put it," he said, nodding. "I'm the free agent here, Sarah. For me, the goal will be to share every moment, however brief. This thing that's happened between us. You have to admit, it's a miracle. The question now is…"

Suddenly, she became silent, obviously pondering. Then she turned to him.

"Let's not push the envelope, Harvey. We're alter kockers and that's the truth of this. This whole bubbameister could be an illusion, something made up by memory and fantasy. Yes, I know what I feel, darling. I feel like someone is supposed to feel if they're more than six decades younger. Maybe it's something we miss, something we remember, and we're just making believe it's happening. In love at our age? Really, Harvey? And this! Two old bodies pleasuring each other. Maybe we're some kind of nature's weirdos. To younger people, what we've been doing here would seem bizarre, outlandish, a kind of freak show. Look at us. Tell you the truth, Harvey. I don't trust it. Not yet, anyway. Worse, I can't do anything about it as a permanent arrangement. Even the idea of permanent at our age sounds crazy. A few days ago, my future was carefully prescribed. Who knew? Maybe what we see is all we get, a clandestine affair."

"I'm not going to overanalyze it, Sarah. So let's not lose ourselves in explanations or logic. Frankly, I hadn't banked on this complication with your husband, and I suppose I must be sympathetic and understanding. I'm not really. Every second counts as far as I'm concerned. I want to spend every waking minute with you. That's my definition of what love is, Sarah. Access." He paused and kissed her neck. "But I will submit to anything you say. Hopefully we can find the time to meet. Frankly, Sarah, I'll settle for every crumb. You set the pace, darling, and I'll follow your lead." He pointed to Ben, sleeping peacefully on the floor beside the couch. "Like him."

She was lost in thought for a few moments.

"I won't press you. I promise," he said, immediately aware of the statement's infidelity. Of course, he would press her. It would be his mission. Wasn't he a master of persuasion? Nevertheless, he felt awful about the dissimulation, rationalizing it as a necessary white lie. He was determined not to let this opportunity pass him by.

"Please don't," she whispered as if she had read his mind. "I beg you. Accept it. The guilt will be corrosive and destroy what we have found."

He nodded, reached for her hand, and kissed her palm. He knew she had a point. She met his gaze for a brief moment and sighed, then nodded and turned away.

"I love you, Sarah," he whispered.

"And I you," she whispered, kissing him lightly on the

lips. He noted that her eyes were again filled with tears.

"Wee wee time," she said abruptly as she sat upright.

He pointed the way to the bathroom, and she padded toward it.

Waiting for her return, Harvey reflected on what had just occurred between them. It was beyond his wildest imagination. It had happened so fast, their meeting, the ups and downs of uncertainty, the sudden explosion of emotion, and its baffling apparent mutuality.

He was, frankly, astonished. Despite their age, they had performed as lovers. He felt manly, proud, potent, viable, involved, still in the ballgame. He wanted to offer a victory yelp. He was in love. He had expressed that love sexually. Her response was beyond his wildest expectation.

Anne, he knew, was far less interested in sex, and often, he suspected, she faked her pleasure. For her, he felt like sex was always a chore, although essential to validating their marriage. Toward the end, they had pretty much abandoned it.

"Penny for your thoughts," she said as she returned, sliding beside him on the couch, insinuating her arm under him.

"Is it a sin to be so happy?"

She chuckled. "That is so Jewish," she said, "to feel guilty when you're happy."

"Well then," he joked. "You must be smothered in guilt."

"I should be, I suppose. For eating trafe."

"Trafe?"

"Non-kosher."

"Do Jews get punished for that?"

"Maybe," she laughed, looking toward the ceiling. "Forgive me, God. I fucked a goy. It's a mitzvah."

"Meaning?"

"A blessing."

"I'll buy that," he replied, growing thoughtful. "Now what?"

"Ich vased."

"Meaning?"

"How should I know?" Then she drew in a deep breath. "I told you my story, Harvey. I'm locked into a situation I never expected."

"Nor did I."

"Don't look for resolution, Harvey." She became lost in silence. He continued to caress her breasts. She chuckled suddenly. "You are so far out of my orbit."

"Am I? As I told you the other day, opposites attract. All I know is that I love you. I want you near me. I need you. Above all, I do not want to miss the moment. The train could leave the station at any time."

"Don't make me mishugana, Harvey. It is what it is. "

They kissed deeply again, then disengaged. He whispered in her ear, "I don't ever want to be alone. Not anymore."

"I wish," she sighed, dead serious now. She turned her arm and looked at the time.

"I hate being on the clock," he said.

"Me, too," she sighed, frowned, and avoided his eyes. "I'm trapped, Harvey. Committed. I beg of you. Don't push me on this. It will destroy anything we have together. Please, Harvey, if there is anything real between us, if we are..." She pursed her lips, took a deep breath, and then continued. "If we are in love, accept the situation. I'm a tough old bag, and when I commit, I commit. I owe this to Frank, to our life together, to our past."

"Is that some Jewish thing?"

She frowned and seemed puzzled.

"Jews are always talking about high moral gestures," he explained.

"Are they?"

"I meant it as a compliment," he said, obviously noting her sudden displeasure.

"Jews don't take it as a compliment, Harvey. It smacks of believing that we're superior to thou, if you get my drift."

"I hadn't meant it as an insult, darling. I have enormous respect for you people."

"Us people?"

"Yes, for Jews. Think of what you have accomplished."

"You mustn't pander, Harvey."

"I'm so sorry, Sarah. Really. It has no relevance to my feelings for you. If I've said the wrong thing, then teach me, caution me. Nothing must come between us, darling. I love you. That's all that matters."

"Maybe I'm being too sensitive," she acknowledged.

"Not at all. Guide me through the minefields, darling. "

"I'm having trouble enough finding the way myself."

He sensed that the brief antagonism had dissipated.

"The issue with caring for my husband is a matter of obligation. I owe him that. I took an oath. In sickness and in health. Till death do us part."

He nodded, realizing that he had taken the wrong tack. He retreated.

"I'm not asking that you abandon him, only upgrade his care by professionals."

"I have a professional on my payroll," she shot back. "She believes she is doing God's work."

"God's work?"

"Easing the exit. If she thinks God is pulling the strings and she is the rep, okay with me." She shrugged and chuckled. "Maybe we can get her to put in a good word for us on longevity."

"Actually, he seems to be doing a pretty good job of it so far." He put his mouth on her breast and tongued a nipple.

"No kinahora. It's bad luck."

"Kinahora?"

"Means bragging about good luck."

He was somewhat confused. Jews and their strange superstitions, he mused. But longevity was much on his mind lately, and meeting Sarah had heightened the issue. Nothing was forever, and there was a time limit on everything, especially people. He wanted to ask her what message her caretaker had from God about how long it would be before her husband got to his marching orders, to wherever his spirit or corporeal body was destined.

From what he had learned casually, dementia or Alzheimer's could go on for years. Had they the time to wait it out? He was tempted to ask her for an estimate but feared offending her. Of course, that was the central question.

"So you're destined to be my afternoon lay," he said, regretting it instantly. She shrugged but did not seem to take offense.

"Until circumstances change," she said emphatically.

He grew thoughtful over a long moment of silence. His mind was spinning.

"Look at us, Sarah. We found this needle in a haystack—you and I. It's one in a trillion. Two survivors. Still viable. That's what we are, Sarah. Is this relationship destined to be merely a series of afternoon trysts?"

"No more, Harvey."

"Sorry." He berated himself. Wrong tack again. He must avoid the obvious, opt for subtlety. His mind searched for other possibilities.

"I have a question," she asked, breaking a long silence.

"Fire away."

"You are obviously a viable man sexually. Why me, an old bag, when you could probably attract some younger babe? Say, someone 40-ish or even younger. Done all the time. Hell, wouldn't you welcome some younger, hard body to administer to your obviously still active libido?"

"And what would we be talking about after? It's all about demography. We've lived our lives through the same time frame. Nothing beats points of reference. Sharing the same lifetime pew is essential."

"Jews don't do pews," she snickered. "Not in the sense you meant."

"You know what I mean. And by the way, why would a viable sexy lady like you fancy an old guy like me when she still has the equipment to tempt a younger guy to coax multiple performances to satisfy her hankering?"

"Hankering? Did you hear that in an old Gary Cooper flick? And I don't want to explain to some younger guy who Gary Cooper was."

"Or Betty Grable."

She caressed him.

"You like that, Harvey?"

"Beyond like, darling."

"Frank's caretaker does that to Frank. She says it comforts him."

The context had obviously returned her thoughts to her current dilemma of coping with her husband's illness. He tried to steer it in a more compatible direction.

"Is that supposed to be God's instructions as well?"

"Must be."

"Explains why he invented Eve. "

"Or he was worried that Adam's hand was getting tired."

He laughed. He loved her wisecracks, her often raunchy humor, the give and take, their snappy dialogue, the wit. Sadly, it had not been Anne's forte.

He continued to dwell on the tactics he must employ to make their relationship permanently full time. To everything there was a solution. He had learned that in the ad business. If one tack didn't work, try another. The fact was that he hated the idea of accepting her conditions. Obviously, her thoughts were concentrating on her current dilemma, mulling over the peculiar details of her ordeal.

"I suppose she wanted my permission to do this. The patient and his needs are her priority. She has her own view of the protocols. Her objective is to ease the suffering as much as possible. It is a tough job to live up to her expectations for loved ones. Fact is that anything that comforts Frank is okay with me. She is a godsend."

"God again," he muttered. "An idea with legs." He was reverting back to his advertising lingo.

So I am competing with a dying man and a guardian angel, he thought. Logic was on his side. Their version of conscience and compassion was on theirs. Suddenly he was assailed by what was, under ordinary circumstances, a terribly cruel thought. He wanted her husband to hurry up and die.

"It's the old cliché, Harvey. Life isn't fair."

"That doesn't cut it at our age, Sarah. Fairness doesn't apply."

"What does?"

"Life is not a permanent condition. That's a fact, not a cliché."

He regretted his own sudden tone of rebuke. After a long silence, she stirred.

"I just can't," she sighed.

"There are places," he persisted. "They provide expert care."

She mulled over his comment. Her nostrils twitched. "We don't abandon our wounded."

"So now you're a Marine," he shot back.

She shrugged and offered an amused chuckle. "Let's drop it for now."

"Only for now," he pressed, "or what is left of now."

"You mustn't make it difficult, Harvey. At least we have this, boobala." She caressed his cheek.

He watched her slip into a long, reflective silence, observing her contemplating the dilemma that was, beyond all reason, conflicting both of them. This was a completely unexpected issue that had appeared in their lives at the wrong moment. One might characterize it as the last moment.

His penchant for advertising slogans, a skill that dominated his entire career, rolled into his mind, triggering his imagination. Finding love a minute to midnight. The almost happy ending. Last chance for love. Love's grand finale. How many ways were there to encapsulate their situation?

"Alright," he said breaking the silence. "What would you suggest?"

She nodded but remained silent. He speculated that she might be searching for some way to express herself without harming this odd but overwhelmingly powerful thing between them, as if she were somehow carrying delicate porcelain and feared breaking it. Of course, he could be wrong about what she felt and what she pondered.

"Future events will sort it out, Harvey."

"Meaning?"

"Life's ending has no sell-by date," she whispered. "I'm committed, Harvey. I'm sorry."

"Every minute away from you, Sarah, will be lost. And there aren't that many minutes left." He paused and watched her expression.

"I just can't go there, Harvey. Not again. We're getting repetitive," she sighed.

She disengaged and stood up, then gathered her clothes and began to dress. Shafts of light had dimmed, and she clicked on a lamp. He watched her dress. She looked toward him, smiled, and opened her arms.

"What you see is what you get," she said, shrugging. "I'm not the teenage beauty of your fantasy life."

He stood up and repeated her gesture, exhibiting his own still naked body.

"Who is?"

He moved toward her, and they embraced again.

"You looking for a paragraph in the medical journals?" she asked. "Or are you just being a show-off?"

They giggled and disengaged, deliberately off topic now. She finished dressing and looked at her watch. Ben, who had been snoozing, suddenly awoke and shook himself.

"You should take lessons, Ben," she said.

She went off into the bathroom while Harvey dressed. She wasn't long. She looked at her watch.

"We could wake up from this fantasy, Harvey, and all this could disappear in a puff of smoke. Does anything really happen at this speed? It's like," she paused and grew thoughtful, "like when you wake early and fight your way back to sleep, then suddenly dream in what seems like real time, only it's not real time because it encompasses what appears like days in which crucial life-changing events happen, and then you are awake all of a sudden, and you discover that the so-called dream took all of ten minutes."

"And you think this is what we are experiencing?" Harvey wondered.

He was confused and noted a touch of belligerency in his comment. His response was to draw her to him and kiss her deeply.

"Are you saying this is not happening?" he asked, breathless, oddly frightened. "That it's like that quick compressed dream. Unreal?"

"I never said unreal, darling."

"It's the most realistic thing that ever happened to me," he said. They kissed again, and then she squirmed out of his embrace.

"If I can get a cab, I will escape the wrath of Brunhilda," she said.

"And God."

At the door, they kissed again and then disengaged. "What about one for the road?" Harvey offered. But without another word, she was gone. He looked at Ben who returned his gaze with expectation.

"Don't look at me like that, kiddo."

Ben's tail wagged in response.

"I'll figure it out. Don't I always?"

Ben lied down again and put his snout between his paws.

"One for the books, Ben. You gotta admit."

Ben closed his eyes.

Later, Harvey's mind roamed back to advertising mode. Yes, he thought. Love at twilight. That would work. He looked toward the blinds and wondered how an artist might creatively depict a silhouette of a man and a woman, their naked flesh lit by a tiny sliver of the fading rays of the sun.

He saw it in his mind's eye and felt tears of happiness roll down his cheeks.

6

"Do you remember?" Sarah asked her husband. It was three words that had become a kind of mantra. She had assessed her dilemma in that old cliché that had been floating in her mind, namely that she was being hammered between a rock and a hard place, between guilt and obligation.

"The Cotswolds, Frank. In England. That lovely summer. We stayed in that quaint little inn. What was the town again? We laughed at the name. Stow-on-the-Wold. We stayed at that lovely inn. Remember, Frank? They came to us with breakfast in bed while we were making love, and we told them to come in anyway. What a hoot! Remember, Frank?" She paused, saw a very faint upturn of his lips, a kind of smile that encouraged her to continue. "My God, the look on that girl's face. I saw it, of course, since we were in the missionary position, and you were facing in the wrong direction. She put the tray down on the table beside the bed without cracking a smile, as if this was breakfast as usual. It was a gas. Remember, Frank?"

He looked at her blankly, and his thin smile faded. It was obvious he had no memory of the incident that had once been a hilarious feature of his anecdotal recall.

"Later, we drove around and visited all those antique stores. We bought that big Chinese export plate that we carried home and put on the table in the living room. It's still there, Frank." She pointed to it. "You see it every day." She paused, searched her own memory for more. "Remember, Frank, we went to Bath, and then the next day, we saw *King Lear* at Stratford. You loved it, Frank. You said it was the best *Lear* you had ever seen."

She inspected his eyes for any sign of recognition, but they had retreated to a static, fixed look, exhibiting not the slightest effort at recall. Helena was helping him with breakfast, encouraging him to spoon up his oatmeal. She had instructed Sarah to be sure she maintained eye contact. It was all about encouraging recognition, she had explained, and Sarah had obeyed as usual with ever-decreasing results.

Studying Frank's eyes, she searched for the slightest spark of recognition. Briefly, at the mention of *Lear*, he appeared to smile faintly.

He mumbled a word that sounded like Lear.

"That's it, Frank. It was at Stratford, where Shakespeare came from. That town."

She exchanged glances with Helena who nodded her understanding.

"Shakespeare," she pressed. "You remember Shakespeare, Frank. And *Lear* in the theater at Stratford, Stratford on Avon, and we went back to the inn and had smoked salmon sandwiches in front of the roaring fire."

His eyes flickered briefly as if she was getting through to him, and that encouraged her.

"Shakespeare, Frank. Surely you remember. You knew all his plays. *Lear* was your favorite. Then after. Sure, you remember after, the logs crackling in the fireplace." Her voice rose in frustration. "Dammit, Frank." She wanted to scream it. Helena motioned her to calm down, and she took a deep breath and offered a sigh of futility.

"Are you finished with your oatmeal?" Helena said in a matter-of-fact tone. Frank looked down at the half empty bowl and stared at it. "Good, Frank," she said, removing the bowl and going into the kitchen. Sarah faced her once vibrant husband who looked downward and remained silent.

"It's me, Frank," she whispered, caressing his shoulder. "Sarah, sweetheart."

"Sarah," he mumbled, his expression puzzled. She reached out and clasped his hand, then brought her lips to it.

"Remember, Frank, all those protest marches? We stood for something Frank, didn't we? I'm still out there, Frank, still pushing the agenda. You can't let those right wing bastards win the day. Those fucking Republicans." Again, thoughts of Harvey intruded, and the irony confused her and suggested yet another tack. She debated with herself, looking toward the kitchen where Helena was now rinsing the breakfast dishes.

"Remember, Frank?" she whispered, bring her mouth close to his ear. "Remember, Frank, how we used to have a ball?"

Nothing stirred him. With no warning, she began to sob. Then she cleared her throat and tried again. "And the kids, Frank, remember how we fussed over those two little girls, how happy we were? Our two little girls. I was always telling you how you spoiled them, and you did, Frank. You did. I was the disciplinarian, Frank. You remember, I was a bit overprotective, considering my early days. "

At the memory of her earlier days, she again changed tack. "Try to remember, darling. Please try to remember how broken I was when we met and how you saved me, Frank. You literally lifted me out of the mud, Frank. You saved me. I remember that, and you never let me down, never. Not once in all the years we have been together. Try to remember, darling. Try hard. I need you to remember." She paused and whispered, "Especially now."

Of course, she knew his brain was caught in tangles that would never untwist. His memory was dying fast, but she continued to try, as if a sudden rescue would save her from the temptation presented by her relationship with Harvey. She had this sudden urge to confess to him and say, *I am in love with another man named Harvey. I am unfaithful. I don't understand it. It happened. I love him. I love you, too. I will always love you, Frank. And I will never, never, never put you in the hands of strangers. Open your memory, Frank, and help me battle this new complication. Help me, Frank.*

When Helena returned, Sarah picked up a napkin and wiped her wet cheeks and feigned a cough. By then, Frank had turned away and was looking at the television screen. The sound had been turned down. Helena turned it up, and Frank's eyes engaged with the black and white movie in progress. It was a Fred Astaire, Ginger Rogers movie. They had both loved these stars, especially when they danced together.

"See, Frank. Fred and Ginger." She cleared her throat and pointed to the screen.

"Fred and Ginger," he mumbled and nodded as he watched the dancing couple. Sarah tried to concentrate on the movie, but her tears clouded her vision.

"Forgive me, Frank," she sighed, turning her thoughts to Harvey and their so-called clandestine affair. The images that popped into her mind brought even more conflict and guilt—and need. She wanted to fall into Harvey's arms.

It had been three months since that first glorious encounter in the park between Sarah and Harvey. They had met daily in the park and three times a week at his apartment since then. Intimacy between them had grown along with the complexity of their relationship and what had become an increasing dilemma of timing.

They met during her yoga time, and soon she had even abandoned most of her extracurricular advocacy meetings. When she was away from him, she longed to be with him, but however subtly and sometimes openly he pressed her for more time together, she resisted.

She acknowledged that she was genuinely and passionately in love with him. It was no longer simply miraculous. It had become a way of life.

Harvey had lived up to her sexual expectations, helped by medication, although there were moments of temporary failure that mostly she managed to assuage. For her part, she valiantly tried to make peace with the status quo and pursued her routine with stubbornness, although the constrictions between her sense of obligation to Frank and Harvey were making her increasingly tense.

She questioned her greedy pursuit of pleasure and floated among guilt, selfishness, and surrender. She often felt in the grip of some irrational madness, an escape from the terror of her husband's involuntary and incurable withdrawal from reason and awareness. Had she the right to pleasure while his mind faded into darkness and oblivion? It became an obsessive debate within her mind.

And yet she knew it was not simply the pursuit of pleasure. It was passion, love, however defined. How could people their age fall in love and join together in all the accompanying notions of romance?

"I don't believe this," Harvey would tell her every time they met, which was daily in the park, whatever the weather. It was getting colder now, and there were signs of a harsh winter in the offing. Most mornings he would walk the long distance to the West Side, which allowed her more time to be with him. She looked forward to their morning embrace, which energized them both.

Ben, she noted, was growing increasingly frail and visibly slowing down. Shaina was showing her age as well.

"We're acting like teenagers," she would remark often. "And our canine kids are falling apart."

Harvey had informed her that he had taken Ben to his vet, who had offered a gloomy diagnosis. Ben was dying of old age and showing numerous canine health problems. He had hinted at taking Ben out of his misery, much to Harvey's consternation. Shaina, too, was declining, and the condition of both dogs was one of their prime topics of conversation.

WARREN ADLER

By then, their so-called clandestine affair had intensified. In addition to their morning meetings in the park, they called each other frequently, but only at set times. Declining dexterity, an acknowledged problem for both of them, made it difficult for complicated texting, and most of their communication was by voice. Above all, Sarah did not want to attract Helena's attention, although she doubted that Helena would mention it as long as nothing interfered with the rituals she had established for her patient.

There was no question in Sarah's mind that Helena would soon have to move into their apartment full time. The nights alone with Frank were getting more and more troublesome, and Sarah's lack of sleep was making her irritable, leading to outbursts that she instantly regretted.

Harvey continued to press her to take steps to relieve her burden and come live with him. Indeed, there were moments that she felt her stonewalling beginning to crumble and other moments when she was stubbornly resistant. As their love bond strengthened and the pleasures and intensity of their affair deepened, the issue persisted as Frank's situation worsened. At times, she made a half serious effort to project denial in a lawyerly rebuttal.

"We would never be compatible over the long term, Harvey. We are oil and water in numerous areas. You are the embodiment of everything I have been opposed to all my life." In trying to work out a convincing argument, she would count off the negatives. "Look at you. A conservative, a Republican, yuk, a goy, and every Jew in their hearts know that all goys are likely to be genetically anti-Semitic. Okay that's a bit harsh, but there's lot of history and truth in the assertion. It follows that as a conservative, you have no compassion for the poor, the downtrodden, the underprivileged, and are against using the government as a source to help them and be a kind of seed bank to grow these unfortunates into self-sufficient citizens. You are allied with causes that emphasize selfishness and are designed to maintain the status quo. You hate government and live in some fantasy that less government is the best government. You're also a Kansas hick and hate Democrats, especially lefties like me. And don't think I can't see into your subtle manipulations to get me to put my husband into some kind of home, get him out of the way, to give you a clear field to scoop me into a live-in situation. I'm onto you, Harvey. You can't fool me. What you really want is for me to throw Frank under the bus, discard 50 odd years of marriage, devotion, loyalty, sharing, decency, obligation. No way, José. Jews don't do that. No way."

"Are you saying it is some kind of Jewish thing?" It was part and parcel of his usual rebuttal, but usually went no further. She sensed his caution on the subject and respected it. Although she believed in it profoundly, the claim of moral superiority by Jews was a toxic assertion by non-Jews.

Harvey responded to her characterization of him with an undercurrent of mirth and gentle diplomacy, playing what she termed the guilt card.

"You must understand, my darling. All those characteristics you cite are clichés that have run out of power. Timed out. We need all our energy for the finish line. Everything else is done and gone. Over. All my energy is concentrated on one single premise, and that is that I love you. I want to spend all my remaining days with you. I want to see your face every day of my life. Hear your voice. Love you in every way, physically as long as I can. I just want to be in your proximity, in your presence, every second of every minute of every day. All those differences you cited. Maybe they once existed. Maybe not. Who cares? We are both in a different place. My darling, please understand. We are just a couple of minutes to midnight, and I want to treasure every moment before the 12 bells toll. No, I am not a blank slate, but nothing beyond my love for you has any relevance at this point in time. Everything else is autobiography. All I want to do is write the last chapter."

"Great metaphor, darling, but unfortunately, I'm still on the next-to-the-last chapter."

"Time to close it then. You've run out of text."

"Unfortunately, not yet," she would sigh. It had become for them a perpetual debate, ending always at the same place.

Their assignation in Harvey's apartment had taken on a routine of its own. They met three times a week in early afternoon and spent most of the time in bed. They were both aware that true companionship required more, the normality of a lasting relationship, a social compact, a marriage, however defined. At this stage, they both saw themselves as lovers, locked into, as he would describe it, an endless clandestine affair.

Of course, he wanted permanence, a fool's definition in itself, and as she often acknowledged, he had every right to desire it. His argument was always grounded in time and its passing, hers in obligation and commitment. It was a never ending roundelay between them.

At home, she performed her duties as a devoted, caring wife determined to fulfill her sacred obligations to her husband. She felt absolutely certain he would have done the same for her. At about the four-month mark of her relationship with Harvey, she arrived back at her apartment and confronted Helena.

"How long?" A sudden panic seized her and seemed to inhibit her speech. She and Helena exchanged glances.

"Only God knows, Mrs. Silverman." That was the question that now rattled around in her mind, especially after these odd diatribes during her visits with Harvey.

"I thought you had a direct line, Helena."

She was getting increasingly testy but also wary of crossing the line. Helena was her savior, her godsend. At this

point, it was beyond argument, and she had by then constructed an aura of truth around the assertion. God was
watching them. Only God knew the answer.

"God knows but never tells. Some have been known to
linger for years."

"Years?"

"As you know, there are stages that are predictable. But
the timeline is less accurate. People progress differently.
My advice is, as I've said to you many times before, is to
take it day by day. In the end, only God decides."

Sarah felt her insides tighten and knew its source. What
she now called the Harvey issue was threatening the resolve
of her commitment. Resisting it, she challenged herself to
dismiss it. A once-memorized childhood poem suddenly
reverberated in her mind. It had done so in her heyday in
the 1960s when it had perfectly described and rationalized
her life's excesses.

Gather ye rosebuds while ye may,
Old Time is still a-flying;
And this same flower that smiles today,
Tomorrow will be dying.

As she recalled it, her heartbeat accelerated, exacerbated
by the fact that Helena was watching her.

"Are you okay, Mrs. Silverman? You're white as a sheet."

"I'm fine, Helena," she managed to say, turning away
quickly as she felt her eyes tearing up.

Harvey had grown more sophisticated in his food offerings, and he continued providing Champagne, discovering
that the buzz seemed to stimulate their sexuality, despite
the warning that alcohol was not a good mix with Viagra,
for which he now had a more than adequate supply. Thankfully, the Viagra seemed to help.

Most of their time together was now spent in his king-
sized bed where they shared a constant dialogue, reflecting
on their current concerns and conflicts. They had vowed

transparency to each other, holding nothing back. Their conversations, as they had both acknowledged, became a living memoir of their long and varied lives, often punctuated by tears and laughter.

Harvey often acknowledged that Sarah's life had been far more adventurous than his. She characterized his life as the gold standard of respectability, a typically conservative life in waspland.

"Okay then," he would respond with amusement. "Give me a shot at the gold standard of adventure."

She greatly enjoyed the telling and sensed that he was mesmerized by her stories, especially those of her wild early days.

"I wish I had experienced that," was his regular rejoinder.

"The living of it was beyond a doubt one of the most fabulous experiences of my life. But the crash ending was a nightmare," she admitted. "Thankfully, Frank was there to rescue me."

"Hence your current payback," he would add.

"Hence my current payback," she would acknowledge.

"My cross to bear," he would sigh often, knowing it would set off discussion.

"An apt image for people of your persuasion."

"My persuasion? Meaning the tight-assed wasp stereotype?"

"Something like that."

"And you give us no credit for conceiving and establishing the foundation for this country."

"Many of whom were slaveholders."

"They were men of their times."

"Note the gender."

"I do. *Vive la différence.*"

She arrived at his apartment always greedy for stimulation, conversation, and sharing. And sex. Every discussion was amplified. Nothing was held back. Deep intimacy and total transparency seemed necessary, a substitute for direct experience.

"I've always been strongly sexed, darling," she had explained. "But this late-life desire is a gusher. I don't know why. It must be you."

"I hope so," he replied, but his statement lacked conviction. "But you are a phenomenon in that area."

"I have no basis of comparison," she would respond coyly.

He had learned to pace himself, he told her, knowing that a climax for him would end any possibility of insertion. Indeed, they were both completely open about their sexual capabilities, and she marveled at their willingness to be transparent about their feelings, their defects, their fears, their aspirations, their past glories, their mistakes, and their joint arrival at a moment in their lives when their secrets and strategies were totally uncensored.

While he articulated how deeply he loved and desired her, he was obviously aware of the limitation placed on his sexual performance by age. He admitted to her that the depletion of his energy increased his need for longer naps. The pleasure, he told her, was still strong, and he acted as a dutiful and compliant lover, but his efforts, as he had discovered, hardly compared with the sheer power of her miraculous and still formidable sexuality.

"I admit," he told her often, "women are the stronger gender. By far."

"Another of God's jokes. The proof is that we live longer."

"I've been trying to make that point. Hence my sales pressure."

"Stop noodging, Harvey."

She had explained what noodge, or nudge, meant among her endless yiddishisms.

Occasionally, he would experience a faltering, but she

became so well attuned to such events that patience, understanding, and skill on her part managed to happily bridge the gap.

What mystified him, he often admitted, was the equation between love and sex that had always been murky in his mind. Sex for him, he explained, had somehow been detached from love, a kind of add on, an obligatory validation as it had been for him and Anne and for his infrequent dalliances, a kind of brief and pleasurable recreation.

He told her that discovering such a sexual relationship in old age was a revelation, an enlightenment, an activity that was generally deemed by the popular culture as an aberration. Talking about it, they both discovered, was part of the fun.

"I am a dirty old man," he would exclaim in the midst of their afterplay, especially when they were slightly buzzed on Champagne, which had become their drink of choice during their times together.

"Such a mitzvah," she would counter. "Helena would say I was doing God's work."

"How so?"

"Testing the limits of his creation. After all, he was not too happy with his first tries. He killed most of them off in a flood."

"But he kept samples to try again."

"You learn that from goyim Sunday school?"

"Bet they cleaned it up first."

"Now you're giving Bible lessons."

He could not contain his laughter, and she joined in, settling finally, then pursuing the subject.

"Then his son saw Noah drunk and balls-ass naked with a woody," Sarah blurted.

"Get her," Harvey would reply with an elbow jab. "She walks the walk and speaks the talk."

They loved it, slightly high, being silly, playing word

games, tickling, fooling around, teasing, imitating, making funny sounds, rediscovering childhood frivolity, letting go. An observer would have corralled them and sent them to a funny farm. They would exhaust themselves with laughter.

"Who are we?" he would shout.

"Two dumbass broken down old farts fucking around."

"You think God is watching?"

"Hope so," she would cry, casting her eyes toward the ceiling and spreading her legs. "Take a good look, God. It's still in business. Thank you, kind sir."

They would erupt in hysterical laughter after such antics.

She would often tell him that she always thought that uptight Republican goys from the Midwest had no sense of humor, that they went to the now extinct Stage Deli and ordered cream cheese and jelly sandwiches and thought corned beef was a steak buried in corn kernels and a knish was a Jewish doughnut. Laughter, she knew, was yet another dimension of their relationship.

But while the sexual and letting go part was a component of their life together, the time spent was primarily one of deep communication between them, moments of intimacy filled with revelation, personal histories, anecdotes dredged from memories of their past lives. It soon occurred to both of them that they were indulging in an exchange of mutual autobiographies, the raw, uncensored truth of what each of them had experienced in their more than eight decades of life.

Toward the end of their moments together, they would lie in bed, relaxed, sated, their minds floating on a river of revelation. Hours would pass between them, a free-for-all of revelation without barriers, the raw truth of a life lived and still in progress.

"Odd," Sarah told him when the subject found its way to their progeny. "How our children drifted to faraway places, geographically, emotionally, so far away from what we once contemplated. My Sheila is the reincarnation of Joan of Arc. She's adopted all the humans on the planet, treats her parents like some go-between that made her, grew her, sent her off to save mankind. Go figure."

"And the other?" Harvey asked, shifting gears, clarifying. "The lesbian?"

"Please don't identify her by her sexual orientation. I am okay with it."

"To each his own," Harvey said, his repetitive paean to tolerance.

"I guess it's a generational thing. Man, woman, children. Say what you want. That was always the natural equation, but then, you and I both know the illogic of love. Why us? Why this man or woman or not that man or woman? Genders apart or together. I am not judgmental." She paused. "That's not true either. I am judgmental. Everyone is judgmental, even if they deny it." She grew silent, pondering. "Don't we have to accept what we cannot change?"

"I'm agreeing, of course," he said in a deliberately formal tone. "Have you told them about us?"

"No way."

"Wouldn't they be happy for you?"

"They would probably think in their gut that I have deliberately abandoned their father."

"Whom they rarely see."

"I'm giving you the emmis, Harvey."

"I'm not sure I love my son," he countered unexpectedly. Had he ever said that to anyone before? He was deeply proud of what he and Anne had created from their bodies. Was it achievement and pride in the very idea of the power of creation? He had been devoted and protective, following the path of his own parents, and he was certain they had loved him. So what of his son? It prompted an explanation of his current relationship with his son, the issue of money and the limits of his fatherhood obligation. He and Sarah spent much of their time together deciphering the obligations of parenthood and how it impacted them.

"As we walk the last mile," he told her, "it is only us, just us. Hand in hand, step by faltering step. Just us." Of course, they both knew it wasn't totally true. There was also Frank.

It was not all fun and games between them. Sometimes she could not contain her political views, mocking him and his ancestors.

"I don't suppose you wasps understand, having ruled the roost in America from the beginning."

"I'd better steer away from that one, Sarah."

"Not your fault, darling. Your fucking sense of entitlement is in your genes as well."

Early on in their relationship, she had defined *emmis*. He acknowledged that he fell in love with the word as she had defined it.

"It means the absolute unvarnished truth," he told her. "For us, that is the icing on our cake. The emmis. No holds barred. No little deceptions. No lies. Not even the white ones. We are true to one another, darling. Do you realize that we reveal more to each other than if we had lived together for a lifetime? Do you realize how fantastic that is?"

He told her that she had expressed exactly what was in his own mind, a validation of what was happening between them.

"That's the best part," he acknowledged. But she knew what the worst part was, for both of them. The loneliness when they were physically apart. Although they talked by phone, it was not the same. All the senses were needed for true communication, despite all these newfangled wonders of technology. The fact was that Frank in his current state, Helena, and even Sarah's two daughters were passing shadows, and not the kind of communicants that might offer real intimacy. In Harvey, she had found it, but at the moment, it was impossible to realize its full potential. Indeed, she knew she was settling for half a loaf.

"Would the Gentile issue bother all these people?"

His comment surprised her. "Not that generation. They don't give a shit."

"And you, Sarah?"

She raised herself on her elbow and gazed into his eyes.

"Hell, Harvey. I'm in your bed. I love you. I really, really love you."

"It's not an issue, then?"

"Are wasps that insecure?"

"You do continue to make that reference," he told her gently.

She thought about it for a long moment.

"You got a point, Putz. Maybe I was just teasing." She giggled. "My sensitive boobala. You're beginning to sound Jewish."

"Are Jews supposed to be more sensitive?"

"Why suddenly are these things on your mind?"

"I don't know," he paused, his expression puzzled. "Maybe I'm scared that these issues matter more than they do and could tear us apart."

"They won't. Trust me. Stop overanalyzing."

He lifted his head to observe a sleeping Ben beside the bed. She followed his gaze.

"What do you think dogs dream about?" Harvey asked, obviously changing the subject.

"Sex, maybe," she laughed.

"At his age?"

She turned toward him and tickled his ribs. Time to eschew the serious, she thought, and turn to autobiography. She had characterized it as playing catch-up, a kind of summary of the early chapters of their stories.

"I love being here with you, Harvey. Being open, revealing, confiding, especially filling in the blanks of more than eight decades. I'll bet if we were 50, 60 years younger, we would have fucked five times by now."

"You're giving me too much credit."

Their afterplay conversations, of course, were not always about sex, although it was a powerful component, and she wondered if it was true for everyone, especially those who had attained their age. If so, it was a well-kept secret.

She reviewed her life as a hippie, the way of life, the drugs, the protests, the attitude, the life of no discipline, no restraint. "It was a life of anything goes, unrestrained, untamed. We were young animals in heat, looking for sensation." She paused and stared into the distance. "And something else."

"What?"

"The whole magillah."

"Magillah?"

"The whole story. Nothing left out. Beginning to end. The truth of everything."

"And did you find it?"

"No way. What you learn is that chapters end, but the story goes on." She smiled. "I loved it. And then I guess I was written out of the narrative."

Ten years, she had calculated, brought her to the edge of physical exhaustion, and then, she was immediately older and less relevant, and the cast of characters had changed. She recounted meeting Frank, and the wonderful early years. Going to Brooklyn Law School. Becoming a lawyer. The good early years of motherhood.

"Frank and I were in sync in every way," she told him. "We believed in the same things. And he was Jewish." She began to laugh, full, high pitched. She turned toward Harvey and kissed him deeply. "I probably never even kissed a Republican. Imagine. I lived my whole life hating Republicans. They were always, in my mind, fascists, brutes, anti-Semites, minority haters, the enemy, selfish, always goyem, and then they were found to be Jewish, traitors, self-hating Jews, the worst of the worst."

"And here you are, bedded down with a Republican goy."

"In my dotage, I'm engaged in proselytizing," she joked.

"I don't hate liberal Democrats," he asserted. "I have lived surrounded by them. In fact, I was very kind."

"As if they were misguided children in need of behavioral modification."

"Mostly I remained silent."

"Hiding your resentment."

"As I've told you in a hundred different ways, it doesn't matter anymore, darling. I am too old for the fray, and my circle is very narrow. Mostly dog lovers like yours truly. Not our battle anymore, right or left. It's all bullshit to me now. My world is you and me."

"That's being selfish."

"Bet your biddy."

"And that expression is old fashioned."

"I love old fashioned. I am old fashioned," he chuckled. "Very old fashioned."

Banter and revelation. Revelation and banter. In between was sex, bonding, loving, friendship, comfort, wonders, and miracles packed into a moment that to her might be called the icing on the cake. So unexpected. So welcoming.

She had steeled herself to be resistant to Harvey's understandable relentlessness. She understood his objective. To have her put Frank away, send him to a facility that took care of patients inflicted with this disease, and take up life with Harvey. It was logical, reasonable, even realistic. It was what she wanted, but only when the time came. Harvey never threatened to break off with her. At times, he retreated. Other times, he was aggressive.

"It is pointless, Sarah. Put him away."

It became his mantra, and he presented every rational argument he could think of. It was repetitive, despite her constant protestations that he desist, that she understood all his ploys. It was futile. But he continued, and she grew used to the rhythm of his persistence. To his credit, he knew when he pushed too far and surrendered. Until next time.

When they had been deep in their relationship for half a year, he showed up once at her apartment building, picking a time when he knew Helena had left for the day. Somewhat shocked, although he had threatened that one day he would "see for himself," Sarah had consented to the front desk man sending him up. At that stage, she seemed to have no choice.

"I need to see the scene of the crime," he told her without irony as he entered her apartment. By then, the strain on both of them was taking its toll. Obviously, he had tried every ploy, every tactic to get her to relent from her commitment. At times, she felt herself surrendering, only to reverse course, much to his obvious disappointment.

The apartment was clearly set up as a kind of hospital ward. Frank was seated in his chair in front of the television set.

"This is my friend Harvey," she said addressing her husband, who did not acknowledge the introduction or turn his head in Harvey's direction.

"Does he understand what is happening on the television?" Harvey recognized William Powell and Myrna Loy in the *Thin Man* series.

"Afraid not."

"Does he know who you are?"

"Sometimes," she acknowledged. Actually, she was lying. He had lost that ability months ago.

Harvey walked about the apartment and shook his head in despair.

"You are sacrificing your life, Sarah, throwing it away."

"I didn't want you to see this, Harvey."

"I had to come."

"Helena starts full-time live-in next week," she told him. "That should be of enormous help, especially at night." She nodded after a long silence. "I still can't do it, Harvey. I'm sorry."

"It's madness, Sarah. Besides, it will break you financially." They had discussed the financial aspects of her ordeal. He had offered to help in every way possible, but she had declined.

"You're nursing a dead man, Sarah."

"As you can see, he's not dead."

"He's breathing, that's true. But it's obvious."

"You should not have come, Harvey."

"I had to see the competition."

"Okay then. You've seen it."

"Please, sweetheart. Relieve yourself of this burden. Put him in the most comfortable place you can find. Spare no expense. Everything I have is yours."

"Keep your voice down. He will hear."

"My God, Sarah. Look at him. He will not understand."

"He can hear."

"Okay. Okay." Harvey lowered his voice. It became a harsh whisper.

"Do the right thing, Sarah. For yourself. For me. Stop this mad exercise in self-sacrifice. I love you. I will love you for the rest of my life. Come live with me. We owe this to ourselves. You must not do this. I'm sure you have had a wonderful life with this man. But he is no longer that man. Please. Please. I will help in every way I can."

"I know, darling. I can't."

He shook his head, his expression one of complete frustration.

He moved toward her and embraced her. Her body shook with sobs.

"He will see," she cautioned. Actually, he was still facing the television set.

"I can't live like this, my sweetheart. It kills me to see you, especially here. This is not a home anymore. Can't you see that?"

"No," she protested. "It is Frank's home. And mine."

"He doesn't know you're even alive."

"Don't do this, Harvey. Please leave. You should never have come."

"Sarah, darling. Why are you wallowing in martyrdom?

"Not now, Harvey. We'll talk about this when we meet tomorrow."

"We've talked about it for months."

"Tomorrow, Frank."

Suddenly she moved toward her husband, bent, and sniffed.

"Please leave, Harvey. We'll talk about this tomorrow. I have to..." She sucked in a deep breath.

"Change his diaper," Harvey said, shaking his head.

"Please."

"I love you, Sarah. You can't do this."

"Tomorrow, Harvey."

She felt him watching her as she moved toward her husband and helped him rise from the chair. Positioning him in a walker, she helped him navigate the room, obviously toward the bathroom.

"Tomorrow, Harvey."

"Tomorrow? How many tomorrows do we have, Sarah?"

She did not turn for a last farewell look.

Once Harvey was inside the elevator, he broke down in tears.

7

Even when winter rolled in fiercely, Harvey and Sarah continued to meet at the dog runs. Dog parents were intrepid. Nothing stopped them from walking their dogs. Later, on those afternoons when they met at Harvey's apartment, he had hot soup and sandwiches sent up, and they would spend their precious hours together in the king-sized bed in his master bedroom.

In midwinter, Harvey saw the face of the enemy. The cold, the natural aches and pains of the aging process, Ben's declining health, the loneliness of coming home to an empty apartment on the days she did not come, the inescapable reality of time passing, and the effect of quickening seasonal darkness all contributed to a growing sense of anxiety.

What he had seen on his unexpected visit to her apartment was the full measure of her martyrdom. It was a watershed moment, and he feared that undue pressure would weaken the bond between them, perhaps break it. He had no choice but to cope with patience and, when they parted, to tolerate loneliness and self-pity.

But the effect on him was profound. Although he assured himself of the logic of his proposal to place Frank in institutional care, he knew in his gut that he was hoping the man would die, arguing with himself that such a hope was one of compassion, not purely self-interest. It was, of course, a blatant lie, and he found himself fantasizing about secretly administering some kind of overdose to hasten the process.

Although he stopped pressuring Sarah, fearing she might end their relationship, he forced himself to maintain complete silence on the issue of Frank. While he pined for her full-time company and attention, he knew better than to in any way challenge her commitment to her husband by threats of leaving her, fearing that her choice might be to consent.

He became convinced that she was wallowing in martyrdom. Again and again it began to surface in his mind as some Jewish thing, recalling memories of old Jewish mother jokes. One of the punch lines lingered, the one about putting one's head in the oven. However, it did not provoke him to laughter.

At night, after Frank had gone to sleep, Harvey and Sarah talked on the phone for hours. Communication between them was one long, unending conversation of revelation. At times, there was phone sex. Perhaps it was a method of escape from the heavy burden she was under, and he obliged her without mutual interest.

She used her various devices. It did not turn him on, which was worrisome, since it hinted at a decline in his libido, a persistent fear. It crossed his mind that it might be attributed to the emotional shock brought on by visiting her apartment and seeing the true circumstances of her plight.

"It's like nourishment for me, Harvey. I need it," she pleaded.

"I know," he acknowledged. "I just wish I wasn't sharing you with a machine."

"'Fraid so, bubala, but then that's par for the course when we are solo. But in my thoughts and fantasies, you play the starring role."

"It would be nice to be there in the flesh. As you have said many times, I'm old fashioned."

"Not my choice, darling. When I touch myself, I imagine you are touching me. Power of the imagination."

It did not happen every time they talked at night. But in their talks, she did hint to him in passing that Frank was growing increasingly difficult to manage. For some reason,

Sarah had postponed moving Helena into the apartment. Harvey didn't press her on it after she turned down his offer for financial help.

Harvey observed, too, that she resisted using him as a crying towel, although she could not completely hide tiny clues about her husband's worsening condition and the prospect of financial hardship. It took all of Harvey's willpower to resist pushing the envelope more aggressively. But he had learned the limits of his entreaties.

Ben's increasing frailty was yet another measure of the effect of time passing, and it added to his tension. Walking to the West Side was taking its toll on Ben, especially on bitter cold mornings when they would start their trek in the dark.

"Sorry, kiddo," he told his dog. "I understand. I'm a bit long in the tooth myself."

Harvey continued to have his semi-weekly lunches with George Hapsworth, but it was obvious from the way George looked that those times at the restaurant would soon come to an end. So far, Harvey had not told George or his son Richard about his clandestine affair with Sarah. It was as if the telling of it might break the bubble of his happiness and somehow interfere with the reality of what in his mind still counted as a miracle.

Richard would interpret the relationship as primarily a threat to his inheritance. George would surely cheer it on because of its sexual component. Beyond those two, there was no one else to confide in, except Ben.

Sarah and Ben had struck up a great friendship, and he always greeted her with his wagging tail of welcome.

"I love this woman, Ben, really. And I'm happy you don't mind her joining the love fest between us."

When addressed, Ben would look at him intently with eager brown eyes and wag his signature tail of approval.

"I knew you'd understand, old buddy. And I look forward

to the day when we're all together full time." Ben always listened with serious concentration when addressed in that special tone reserved for their intimate conversations. "Of course, you'll have Shaina for company, and that should be a plus. It will keep you from being lonely if I spend more quality time with Sarah. Incidentally, Shaina sleeps in the same bed as her mom. That could be a complication. You mustn't be jealous and try to crawl into bed with us. Can I count on you to understand that?"

When he adopted a questioning tone, Ben would cock his head and offer a puzzled look.

"But then I'm being premature," he asserted. "No sense putting the cart before the horse." Harvey chuckled. "I mean before the dog."

His son continued to harass him about money. Apparently, Richard's financial condition was deteriorating. He was breaking up with his wife, which meant he now had to pay for two domiciles and his children's tuition at their pricey English private schools. All of it was pushing him to the edge.

Both of Richard's parents were brought up on the traditional bootstrap belief that dependence in whatever form was a cop-out, meaning that parents, once they had paid for a decent education and perhaps some starter contribution, were no longer obligated to support their children. Anne was more forthright in this view and had established a kind of family rule that Richard must find his own economic path.

Unfortunately, Anne's protocols after her death were blunted by circumstances, mostly because Richard's needy British wife had social ambitions that demanded a bigger front than his son's paycheck allowed. Harvey, despite his repugnance for dependence, was softer toward his son than Anne, and he managed to yield occasionally to his son's remonstrance when Richard's pleas became desperate. Both the giver and the given hated the process that resulted in ever increasing tension and smoldering resentment between them.

From Richard's point of view, the solution was always for Harvey to sell his condo at One Fifth Avenue and seek smaller quarters, sharing some of the sales proceeds with him, even before he expired. As Harvey aged, Richard's demands accelerated.

Before Sarah, such entreaties had come with a dollop of logic since Harvey was moving closer to the statistical endgame. But such logic had little merit ever since Harvey discovered that his hopes for greater longevity had risen considerably.

"Really, Dad, isn't it time you gave it up? You don't need such a large place, and as you told me, I will inherit it anyway. It could easily net three or four million after capital gains. I know you're living on your pension and investments. I'm not asking for the moon. I don't want in any way to interfere with your current lifestyle."

It went on and on, and at times Harvey would, contrary to his late wife's wishes, break down and borrow against his investments and send Richard a check. Of course, what his son didn't know was that Harvey was making plans for the day he and Sarah would be together full time, and he had determined that he was not going to sell his apartment. No way. That was to be their love nest until the end, a prospect he would not erase from his mind.

Of course, there were moments when cold reality intruded. He was heading toward the mid-80s despite the so-called Roman spring he was now enjoying. Try as he might to envision the 80s as the new 60s, he could not get his head around a 10-year time frame ahead. On the other hand, reaffirmed by his interaction with Sarah, he might come close, and he vowed to himself to smother any negativity about that optimistic assessment.

He had always been rigidly disciplined about taking his annual physical, and although his long-time doctor declared him reasonably healthy, he did have some errant digestive problems, evidence of arthritis, and incipient high blood pressure being kept under control by pills. The doctor's response to his inquiries about his blood work readings was "unchanged" rather than simply "normal."

Nevertheless, he did receive a reasonably clean bill of health for, as the doctor put it, "a man of your years." Harvey, while gratified by the diagnosis, was realistic enough to interpret it as "cautionary."

Because his doctor had written him a Viagra prescription, he had revealed that he was still managing an active sex life, much to the doctor's astonishment, although Harvey did not confess the full truth of his passionate love affair. It was as if any revelation to anyone in his ever decreasing circle would jinx the joy of his miraculous situation.

Indeed, there were moments when, despite the losing battle in terms of what he considered his ideal future, he would thank his lucky stars for what he had been granted—love in late life with all the bells and whistles. Such thoughts could sustain him for days until the lonely hours kicked in and he brooded over the missed time together.

Of course, they had established their together moments, and a kind of truce had been established as he and Sarah made the best of it. He had promised to accept the status quo to keep the peace, although both of them knew that the issue was their sword of Damocles.

But even their deliberately sheltered privacy was not immune to unintended consequences.

One day, after they had spent a couple of hours together in his apartment, naked in bed, after sex, their conversation far ranging as always, they heard a rattling at the door. Ben's quick movement announced that someone was entering the apartment.

"Dad!" a voice called out.

"Oh shit, it's Richard," Harvey said, jumping out of bed and running for his robe.

"I had better get dressed," Sarah said, lifting the covers and reaching for her underwear.

"The doorman," Richard said and then began moving quickly through the apartment, arriving at the door of the master bedroom as Sarah stood almost naked beside the bed.

"Dad, I'm so sorry," Richard said. "I told them downstairs that I would surprise you. I do have a key, you know."

"In the living room, please, Richard," Harvey ordered. "I'll be with you in a moment."

He turned toward Sarah. "My fault."

"Your fault? He should have called first."

"This is very awkward," Harvey said to Sarah. "He knows nothing about us."

"He knows now."

He had discussed his relationship with his son in depth with Sarah, telling her about Richard's financial pressures. They had agreed not to reveal their affair to their children, each for their own reasons.

This was not the revelation he had envisioned for his son. In the living room, Richard sat patiently on the couch. He knew the way to the liquor cabinet and had poured himself a shot of Scotch. As Harvey came into the room, Richard raised his glass.

"Good for you, Dad," he said, making hand motions indicating large bosoms.

"You should have called."

Harvey noted that his son was somewhat disheveled and quite obviously drunk, wild eyed, and agitated.

"What's going on?" Harvey asked. It was obvious that Richard was under stress.

"The kids were suspended. Tried to hack the expense, then it imploded."

"Don't you still have your job?"

"Bye Bye, Birdie." He poured himself another Scotch. "They downsized. I didn't make the cut."

"That won't help," Harvey said, nodding to the glass in his son's hand. He remembered the boy but barely recognized the grown man.

"Ropes end, Dad. I'm a bit ashamed about screwing up my life."

Then he shrugged and looked around the apartment.

"Could have saved me, Dad."

"I told you that subject was off limits."

Richard turned and emptied his glass.

"How much are you in the hole, Richard?"

"Lots. And I'm sick and tired of taking from you." He stood up rather shakily. "All I'm asking is what you promised as my inheritance."

"Such promises normally occur upon one's demise, which is not, at the moment, in my immediate plans."

"It would square everything for me, Dad. Really."

"Just tell me how much, Richard. "

At that moment, Sarah, fully dressed, came into the room. She had arranged her hair neatly and put on some makeup.

"This is Sarah Silverman, Richard."

Richard offered a disinterested nod.

"This is a private matter," Richard said with a disinterested smirk, an obvious expression of dismissal.

"If you are uncomfortable, Harvey," Sarah began.

"Sarah is part of my life, Richard. We have no secrets."

"Really, darling," Sarah said.

"Darling, is it?" Richard replied, his sarcasm clear.

"We have plans for a future together, Richard." Harvey made an effort to appear gentle but forthright.

Richard seemed stunned, reaching for the bottle to pour another drink.

"Now I get it," he said.

"Get what?" Harvey asked with a brief look at Sarah.

"Why you won't sell the apartment."

"As a practical matter," Harvey began.

"Stop bullshitting me, Dad."

"Maybe I should go," Sarah said.

"Please, Sarah. You must stay," Harvey responded. "Our relationship gives you the right to know. Richard is going through a crisis and needs my help."

"He's picked a nice way to get it," Sarah blurted out.

"Dammit! Stay out of my business, lady," Richard said, raising his voice.

"That was uncalled for," Harvey declared.

"He has a point, Harvey. For some reason he's got me down as a threat."

"He's a bit screwed up at the moment, Sarah. I'm sorry you have to see this."

Richard became flushed and angry. "Look, I didn't know you had a girlfriend. I suppose she lives here."

"Wrong," Sarah said. "I visit."

"To screw," added Richard.

Harvey glanced toward Sarah and saw her anger gathering.

"Is that meant to be a compliment or an insult?" she shot back.

"It's obvious you have an agenda," Richard said, his words increasingly slurred.

"I do," Sarah muttered.

"Taking advantage of his senility," Richard muttered.

Sara turned to Harvey. "You told me you had a son. You didn't tell me he was a schmuck."

"Guess not," Harvey agreed. "He's obviously not himself."

"And you, Dad? Are you yourself? I see where this is going. Don't you get it? She'll creep into your good graces, use any tactic, including what passes for sex, and worm her way into your pocketbook. Don't be naïve. Silverman, was it? You know these people, Dad. They're all alike. Mom will turn over in her grave."

"Pay no attention to him, Sarah. He's all fucked up."

"You've been hoodwinked, Dad. At your age, who are you kidding? This woman will take you for all you've got."

"Stop this stupidity at once," Harvey ordered, his anger accelerating. He turned to Sarah. "Pay no attention. He's being a fool, and he's drunk."

"I have eyes," Richard persisted. "This Jew bimbo is looking for a meal ticket."

"Dammit, Richard! Stop this at once." Harvey reached over and grabbed his son's arm, pulling him up to a standing position. He was obviously very drunk at this point.

"Let me put him to bed," Harvey said.

"I'm outta here," Sarah said. "I got enough on my plate without this."

"I'm so sorry, Sarah. He doesn't know what he's saying."

Sarah quickly left the apartment, and Harvey took Richard into his old room and helped him into bed.

"Sleep it off, Richard. I'm so ashamed. How could you be so cruel? This woman is my sweetheart, and I want her to be my life's companion." He paused for a moment. "As long as it lasts."

"Got you by the balls," Richard said, falling face down on the bed.

Harvey removed his son's shoes, covered him with a blanket, and left the room. The living room was empty, except for Ben, who looked at him with some confusion, his tail not wagging.

The next day, on the phone with Sarah, all Harvey could say was, "Remember, darling. It wasn't me talking. Believe me, he's remorseful. "

"You mean anti-Semites are remorseful? When did that happen?"

"He was drunk, depressed, his kids got thrown out of school, his wife left him. I'll write him a check tomorrow and send him on his way. It has nothing to do with you and me. I'm sorry you had to see it."

"Harvey, he's a fucking anti-Semite."

"He was drunk."

"Drunk or not, he's a fucking Jew hater. Who filled his head with all that garbage?"

"It certainly wasn't me. He was very sorry after I explained the situation. He wants to apologize. Will you talk to him?"

A long silence ensued.

"If you insist."

Richard got on the phone.

"I'm so sorry, Sarah. I had no idea about you and Dad. Really. I was drunk and very out of line. Can you ever forgive me? I wish you all the happiness. Just forgive me. That's all I ask."

Harvey watched as Richard listened and then put down the phone.

"Is she still on?"

"Hung up," Richard said. "I did my duty."

"I suppose I got my money's worth."

He had given Richard a check and asked for the apology in return. He suspected it would be a bad bargain, but he felt caught between a rock and a hard place. He knew he was further alienating his son, but he felt he had no choice. Sarah had once disregarded remarks like this by citing the old childhood refrain, "Sticks and stones may break my bones, but words will never harm me."

"Words matter," he had countered, referring to his life's work in the persuasion business. This incident and her inflammatory reaction proved his point.

"You could have warned me, Dad," Richard said when he had sobered up and prepared to go back to London.

"It required no warning, Richard," Harvey contended. "We've fallen in love. Sarah means a great deal to me. We have this obstacle that prevents our being together."

He had gone through the complete scenario, hoping his son would understand.

"You're not seriously considering marriage, are you, Dad?"

"We haven't discussed that."

He knew, of course, Richard's implications. He had been making that quite clear for years.

"We take everything one day at a time."

While he had no desire to break communications with his son, he could tell their relationship was severely diminished. When they said good-bye later that day, he could sense that.

"You should have warned me, Dad," Richard said again as he prepared to leave.

"Probably," Harvey murmured. "Just get it together," he said, observing his son who was pale and hung over.

"Just be careful, Dad," Richard said as he opened the apartment door.

"Careful?" Harvey responded, but by then Richard had closed the door. Harvey looked at Ben, who had turned to his parent. He seemed confused.

"Careful of what?" he said to Ben, who moved toward Harvey to receive a reassuring pat of affection.

One day in midwinter, Harvey got a call from one of George Hapsworth's nurses asking that instead of meeting him at the Century, he might come up to his apartment at the Waldorf Towers. It had been some time since George had postponed one of their Century luncheons because of this or that. He had never acknowledged that it was because of his health. Harvey knew better and expected that one day he would receive this call.

George's apartment was on an upper floor of the Waldorf

Towers overlooking Park Avenue. Harvey found George in bed, propped up on some pillows, sallow faced and cadaverous, his voice weak and wispy. George offered a yellow-toothed smile to his old friend. He was tended by two severe looking, unsmiling nurses who discreetly left his side when Harvey entered his ornate bedroom filled with paintings and antiques.

"All copies, Harv," George had revealed on his initial tour of the elaborate apartment. "Everything you see is phony," he had confided.

"Not you, George. You're the real skinny."

"Hell, I'm the biggest phony in the place."

Beside the bed was a chair, and George directed Harvey to sit. He was wearing pajamas with a repetitive print of colorful balloons, which gave the sickroom of what was clearly a dying man a playful air.

"I did it, Harv," George declared hoarsely.

"Did what?"

"I fucked them."

Harvey was oddly amused but somewhat confused. George nodded and offered a thin smile. Spittle oozed from both sides of his mouth.

"The nurses?"

"You saw them. That should answer your question."

Harvey chuckled and shrugged.

"I did it," George repeated. "I'm checking out with a couple of mil in debt. I fucked my heirs big time. My ungrateful progeny, my ex-wives, and various greedy relatives. All fucked."

"I seem to recall that was your master plan."

"I'm four months behind in rent at this overpriced edifice owned by foreigners, and the banks have been pressing repayment of my line." He offered a crackling giggle. "I'm failing big time, kiddo." Then he started to cough and could barely catch his breath. A nurse came in and watched him until he settled down.

"This is Paddy," George said. "A barrel of laughs. Best bed pan handler in the business, Harv. Gives the worst blow job on the East Side of Manhattan."

The nurse, eyes to the ceiling, in mock exasperation, pursed her lips and shook her head.

"Incorrigible," she unsmilingly retorted. She was thin, almost cadaverous, and middle-aged.

"I'd book her fast, Harv. Knows her shit. Great for checkouts."

"I'll keep it in mind," Harvey said. It was quite obviously part of their routine, a dark comedy vaudeville skit.

"He was one hell of a creative ad guy," George said weakly, addressing the nurse. "Man, we could sell ice to eskimos. We addicted whole generations to bullshit products, right, Harv?"

"That's one way to look at it," Harvey said. He threw a side wink to the nurse. "I thought we simply gave people choices."

"Sugar. We got 'em hooked on sugar, pain pills, nicotine, sleeping pills, the boob tube, alcohol, gas-guzzling new cars every year, junk food, and cigarettes. Boy, did we push those cancer sticks. I'd walk a mile for a Camel. Lucky Strike Green went to war. Chesterfield satisfies. Call for Phillip Morris. We should all be tried for murder in the first degree."

George's sudden rant exhausted him. He closed his eyes, shook his head, and tried to catch his breath. The nurse, who wore a stethoscope necklace, came closer and pressed it to her patient's chest. Then she made eye contact with Harvey. Her expression was dire.

"Not too long," she whispered as she left the room. Harvey noted that she left the door open and sat just outside within earshot.

"We did some good things, George," Harvey said, deliberately lightening the mood. Hadn't he always been the voice of reason where George was concerned? "We exposed them to the better life."

It struck him suddenly that he had been, always, the steady hand, the good solid Midwestern boy with a knack for catchy words and slogans. Hadn't he always stood aside while colleagues like George ranted and offered their cynical observations? He had listened, mostly amused, but managed to keep away from subjects that hit raw spots among his colleagues. In an odd way, he especially liked George because he secretly shared many of his friend's firebrand thoughts and ideas. It occurred to him that he had always played it safe. He watched for a long moment as George closed his eyes.

Harvey continued to sit by his friend's side until he opened his eyes again. Then he was overwhelmed with a desire to reveal what was going on inside his own mind.

"I'm in love, George," he blurted out as though he was clearing his throat.

"This is the bulletin you bring to a dying man?" Apparently, his own sarcastic statement sparked an alertness in George. "Love? You put it in and poke it around and take it out. That's love."

"We do that, too," Harvey said.

"You lying bastard," George wheezed.

"Have I ever lied to you, George?"

"You were always too dumb to lie, Hayseed."

"I've listened to your lies for more than 50 years, pal."

"So you have, old buddy," George said, nodding weakly. He was silent through a long pause. "So it's love, is it?"

"I have no one else to tell," Harvey admitted. Except Ben, he thought. "You told me your good news about your financial situation, so I'm telling you mine. What are friends for, George?"

Friends, Harvey thought. Aside from Ben, who was there? Age had winnowed his old associates. Anne had been the social programmer. Now there was Sarah and George. And George was on the verge of disappearing.

"But is it mutual, Harv?" George asked in a hoarse whisper. "If it's not...the pain of it..." He fought for breath. "There is no pain like it. For most of my life..."

Quite suddenly, his eyes teared up and a sob rose from his chest. Harvey had never seen George react like this before. He needed no translation.

"I did once, Harv, long, long ago. I may be a loud-mouthed ornery prick, but I was once in love. I mean the real thing. Only...she didn't love me. In fact, no one ever loved me. No woman, I mean. No sweetheart. No true love."

"Really, George?" Harvey was encouraged to tell George more. He took a deep breath and began to talk. George had closed his eyes.

"Her name is Sarah, and she is committed to her husband who has dementia and is slowly dying." He cleared his throat and looked away. Through the open blinds, he could see the Chrysler building, the blinding sun bouncing off of its fantastic roof. Although it bothered his eyes, he concentrated on it and told his old friend what was happening, the whole story of this so-called affair that had changed his life.

"She's a Jew. A West Side liberal with the agenda in her DNA." He paused. "I don't give a damn. I love her," he chuckled.

George opened his eyes. "Jew, shmew. Why should anyone care? Get over that shit, Harv. There ain't no bias in the graveyard. But love. Pick up your chips and don't look back. As for age," his voice trailed off and he closed his eyes again. "God's fucking joke," he whispered, revealing where Harvey had picked up the idea in the first place. For a moment, George appeared to have lost his concentration. Then he nodded and smiled, showing his row of yellowed teeth.

George did not respond, breathing now with some difficulty, as if his last observation had tired him. Harvey, still immersed in the implications of his relationship, continued his narrative.

"She doesn't want her husband to die in the hands of strangers. They apparently had a pretty good life together. I see her point, but I don't like it. We love each other, George. I'm scared to press her too hard. She's one of those stubborn people who think they're always doing the right thing. You know, George. Liberals. You can't get liberals to ever change their minds."

"Fuck politics, Harvey. Politics is bullshit. Politicians have fucked up the world. We had the best of it."

"It's never going to happen like this again, George."

Harvey felt like they were talking at cross purposes. He was talking about his relationship with Sarah, and George was making general observation about the past and the events they had lived through.

"If you're looking for advice, Harv, you picked a lousy time." George's voice was raspy now, barely audible.

"Who picks the time, George? I didn't pick the time for this."

A long silence in the room followed.

"Go for it, Harvey. Love. You won the brass ring." George sounded like a whimper. "You know what, Harv? Near the end, all differences die. "

"Differences?" Harvey responded.

"We're all in the same leaky canoe." George's voice was barely a whisper, and while Harvey made out the words, he was confused by their meaning.

Harvey turned again to the blinding sun reflecting from the roof of the Chrysler building. He squinted until his eyes teared up. When he turned to his friend again, George nodded and smiled. Then his gaze froze as if he were staring at some object on the wall. It struck Harvey as odd, this sudden fixation. Then George's eyeballs seemed to sink deeply into his sockets as if something had been switched off inside his head.

"Nurse!" Harvey cried, realizing that he had just swallowed the sound of his own voice. Recovering quickly, he cleared his throat and called again, louder this time. The nurse he had met before responded quickly, inspected George's face, feeling for a pulse in his neck, and then removing the stethoscope from her neck and placing it on George's chest.

She listened with deep concentration, shook her head, and then slid George's eyelids closed.

"Over," she whispered, meeting Harvey's gaze.

"Dead?"

She nodded.

"He called it God's joke," Harvey said.

"I've heard that before," she said. "You'd better go. We have work to do."

Harvey felt strangely disoriented and walked out of the room as if in a stupor. He had never seen someone actually expire. Anne had died unexpectedly in the hospital. He had embraced her body, but he did not witness the life force leave her. Nor had he been present when his parents died. A chill washed over him as he left the apartment and in a daze took the elevator down to the lobby.

He walked through the crowded streets in a sort of trance. At one point, he crossed against the light and was cursed by a cab driver. As he walked, he felt his knees begin to buckle and had to lean against the wall of a building to steady himself.

It took him a while to restore his equilibrium, but he could not get George's expiring visage out of his mind. He had simply slipped away, disappearing into what could only be described as oblivion, his ranting voice of protest silenced, his heartbeat stilled, his thoughts obliterated, forever lost. It had happened so fast with barely a whimper.

Harvey managed to recover somewhat and regain his energy for the journey back to his apartment. He felt as if he were sleepwalking, oblivious to sights and sounds, making his way back by rote. Opening the door to his apartment, he was greeted by Ben with what appeared to be weary enthusiasm, not the jumping joy that had welcomed him since puppyhood.

Harvey knelt and kissed his snout, pausing for a long moment as he looked into his brown eyes, which seemed to remind him of George's lusterless orbs at the moment of his demise.

He swallowed hard and could not contain his own anguish, accompanied by a swift bout of hysterical sobbing. Of course, he knew why. He had glimpsed Ben's end, and this sudden breakdown was pure panic. He rose shakily, lifted himself to a chair, and took out his cell phone to call Sarah.

It was late afternoon, and darkness had begun its early descent. Sarah did not answer her phone. He left a voice message.

"I need you, darling. I'm about to call my vet to put down Ben tomorrow morning. Can you come with me? I will need you near me. I beg you as a personal special favor. Please call back, darling."

He tried to text her, but his fingers were too shaky. He did manage two words: I need. He signed off, stretched out on the couch, and closed his eyes. Ben sidled over but could not muster the strength to climb up next to him. He lay on the floor beside him, breathing heavily, whimpering.

"I understand, old friend," he whispered. "Believe me, kiddo, I feel your pain." The vet had warned him that there was only one way out of Ben's dilemma. Harvey had accompanied his other dogs on their journey to oblivion. The trauma had been devastating. But then he had Anne. What he needed now was Sarah. He remembered what George had said. "Jackpot!"

He got out his cell phone and punched in Charlie Brooks'

number. The vet had served them through the lives of all their dogs for nearly 40 years. Charlie was a kind man who loved animals, still practicing into his late 70s. The vet's assistant answered and recognized his voice. She must have sensed why Harvey was calling. In a moment, Charlie was on the phone. Each time Harvey had put down one of their dogs, it had been a traumatic experience. But Harvey knew that this one—Ben—would be the most heartrending. It would be the last time, the last dog.

"It's time, Charlie," he said, unable to squelch a sob.

"I know, Harvey," the vet said soothingly. "But you gave him a good life."

"Other way around, Charlie."

"I understand, Harvey. You know I do."

Anne and Harvey had always caressed and petted their dogs through this process as they fell asleep and painlessly expired. And they had comforted each other. It was a profoundly disturbing moment. Their dogs were not merely pets but members of the family, adored and loved. Then Harvey remembered the experience with Richard. Perhaps he had loved these dogs even more than his child. And they had loved back. Above all, loved back. That had always been undeniable. He would often think of the short existence of their dogs as yet another one of God's jokes. He needed Sarah to be with him at this impending crucial moment in his life. He needed her badly.

"Early, Harvey. Before the office opens for the other patients. Okay?" Charlie said.

Harvey felt the tears well up again.

"It's best, Harvey. No pain, as you know. I'll be ready."

Harvey rose from the couch and filled Ben's bowl. Ben struggled to stand up, sniffed the food, but chose water instead. Harvey bent down and embraced his companion.

"Sorry, pal."

Ben put his snout on Harvey's arm, his breathing difficult. Harvey wondered if he would live through the night.

"You were the best, Ben, the best. Tell you the truth, I'm not sure I can hack it alone. Fact is, I need Sarah now more than ever. Today I saw how easily living things slip away, just disappear."

Tears rolled down his cheeks. His chest shook, and it took him a long time to quiet himself.

After awhile, he returned to the couch to lie down. Again, he tried Sarah, repeating his message multiple times as his tension mounted. His frustration at not reaching her was turning to anger. "Where are you?" he cried into the phone. "I need you."

Then he must have dozed. He awoke in a cold sweat, knowing he had had a terrible dream that he could not remember. Beside him on the floor, Ben was whimpering lowly, his breathing hoarse and obviously difficult.

Later, he mounted the courage to call Sarah again. Again, he left a message.

"I'm putting Ben down tomorrow, Sarah. Could you possibly meet me at my vet's? "He gave her the address of the vet and the time he had scheduled. Suddenly, he felt testy and frustrated. "Never mind. I just feel..." His voice trailed off, and he could not continue. He knew he was handling it badly, feeling lost and vulnerable. He rolled off the couch and lay down on the floor beside Ben, holding the failing dog as one would hold a baby.

"Sorry, old buddy," he cried. "I don't know what I'm going to do without you. Then, strangely, he began an imaginary argument with Sarah. *Who says us wasps aren't emotional? Damn those clichés. I'm hurting, Sarah. I need you. Aren't we supposed to be lovers? Or are we telling ourselves lies? I'm in pain, baby.*

He began to feel deeply hurt. Hell, he hadn't spent a lifetime with this woman. It is, after all, a mere clandestine affair. Don't you get it, he assailed her in his mind, growing increasingly anguished. He tried her number again and then hung up, his anger bubbling up to rage.

Outside, it had gotten dark, and he continued to lie on the floor next to his failing companion.

"It's just not fair," he whispered into Ben's ear. The dog had closed his eyes and seemed utterly exhausted, his body swelling as he sucked in each breath, collapsing as he expelled it.

Harvey fell asleep by Ben's side, staying there all night, barely noticing the hardness of the living room floor. Harvey rose unsteadily early in the morning and began to pace the room. Again, he called Sarah's cell. Still no answer. This time he left no message and lay down on the couch, stretching out one hand to touch the suffering Ben. Periodically he called Sarah's number, finally deciding that her not answering was deliberate. Her phone identified the caller. He looked at the phone and cursed it. "Fuck! Fuck! Fuck!" he cried aloud. Ben barely stirred.

Then it was nearly time. He called his car service to arrange to be picked up. He bent down to pat and comfort Ben. It was then that his anger boiled over and he punched in Sarah's number. When her voicemail message ended and he heard the beep, he began shouting at Sarah, who again had not answered her phone. Internally, he felt a rising tide of hysteria gripping him.

"How could you not respond? I thought you loved me." And then he said the unthinkable, again and again, allowing his rage to boil over with anti-Semitic, anti-Sarah, anti-everything declarations to the woman he both loved and detested right now, the woman who wasn't there in his hour of greatest need.

He hung up, exhausted, and turned to Ben, who was trying to stand up. With effort, Harvey lifted his dog and made it to the elevator. The doorman helped them to the waiting car.

"Sorry about this, Mr. Franklin. Hell, you were a good master."

Tears rolled down Harvey's cheeks as he gently petted Ben who lay beside him on the back seat of the car. His shoulders shook uncontrollably. The vet's assistant met them with a roll cart and helped get Ben into the examining room where they laid the gasping dog on the metal table. The vet, faithful Charlie Brooks, examined Ben manually and with a stethoscope. He looked up and nodded.

"No choice, Harvey. We'll ease the way."

Harvey nodded, unable to speak. He lifted Ben off the table and cradled him in his arms. Tears continued to stream down his face, his shoulders still trembling.

"Sorry, Ben," Harvey whispered as he watched the doctor inject the dog with the lethal serum.

"I hate this part, Harvey," Charlie said. Harvey bent down and kissed Ben's snout. He clutched his torso, feeling the heartbeat slow down and finally grow still. After a few minutes, it was all over.

"We'll take care of things," the vet said, grasping Harvey's upper arm.

"He was my best pal," Harvey whispered. He continued to stare at the now dead Ben and pet his lifeless body. The vet stood aside and let it play out. Finally, Harvey took a deep breath, laid Ben on the table, and, swallowing hard, left the room as if in a trance and walked out to the street.

The rush hour crowds, oblivious to his pain, hurried by to their various appointed rounds. Harvey pondered their indifference, dwelling on his overwhelming sense of hurt and loneliness. As he moved through the crowds, he felt disoriented, deeply depressed and isolated. Hell, he had lost his most loyal friend, his companion, his confidant. What now? He wanted the ground to open up and swallow him, make him disappear, end his thoughts.

He lost all sense of time and walked for hours, oblivious

to his destination. Then he quickly realized he was walking downtown in the opposite direction of his apartment. Ahead loomed Washington Square, and beyond it was the park. He had taken Ben there a number of times to amble in the dog enclosure. He headed toward it, sat down at a nearby bench, and observed the antics of the dogs as they scrambled and played with each other. God, he missed Ben. Dear Ben, he cried to himself, sobbing.

After awhile, he wiped his face with the edge of his coat sleeve and took deep breaths to control his inner hysteria. Soon, he calmed down somewhat, and his thoughts turned to Sarah. He reached for his cell phone and called her number. As he listened, he felt his heart pounding in his chest. There was no answer, but soon her message came on, and he began to talk.

"It was awful, darling, really awful. Putting Ben down has really thrown me. I wish you had been there with me. Now all I have is you. I love you, my sweetheart."

It was only when he put the phone back in his pocket that he remembered his last outburst on his last message. A wave of nausea assailed him, and he could barely breathe. How could he have possibly allowed himself to say such horrible things to her? Worse, it was just about the most hateful, bigoted remarks he could have uttered, unforgivable insults that would defy apology. The words rolled back into his memory.

He had no illusions about its consequences. There could be no forgiveness. He had smashed the vessel that held their love. How could he have said those things? Of all the insults he might heap upon her, those were the ultimate. He knew in his gut that what he had said could never be forgotten or forgiven.

Had he really uttered those hateful words? Perhaps he was merely imagining his anger and frustration in a contrived fantasy. Then he recalled Richard's anti-Semitic remarks and how Sarah had reacted. Was such hatred so deeply woven into their psyche that it had become integral to their thoughts, so deeply embedded in their belief system that it had become a perfectly natural inclination?

Had the clearly hateful rant found the trigger that moved the latent load of bullets in the barrel of the embedded pistol hidden in his mind? The lethal image frightened him since he felt certain that he was not armed in this way. He was not conscious of any internal animosity toward Jewish people. Of course, he knew what others, like Anne and certainly his son, might be thinking, thoughts shared by many. He knew the long history of such prejudice and its consequences. Did he share these views without the insight of knowing?

Such fearful thoughts were exhausting him. He rose from the park bench and started the long journey back to his apartment, miles up Fifth Avenue. As he walked, he tried valiantly to reverse his depressed and defeatist state. He would throw himself at Sarah's feet, explain the paradox of what had invaded his mind, and offer sincere apologies.

When he finally arrived home, he was perspiring, and although he had not eaten, he was not hungry. The silence and the physical absence of Ben was further unnerving him. Despite what had occurred earlier that day, he expected to hear Ben's welcoming bark and his excited greeting. He felt disoriented and unable to focus. Nevertheless, he forced himself to reach for his cell phone, only to discover that it was not charged. He quickly connected it to his charger, removed his clothes, and went into the bathroom to shower, hoping that the rush of hot water might help alleviate his extreme sense of hopelessness.

With his clothes strewn around the apartment, he entered the shower and adjusted the water as hot as he could stand, soaping his body as if it might scrub away his misery. He lavishly soaped his genitals but could not muster the slightest sexual sensation. After a while, he settled on the floor of the shower in a fetal position and let the water run over him, losing track of time. Finally, he rose, got out of the shower, and lay down on the bathroom floor, stretched out on a pile of towels. He must have dozed briefly. When he awoke, chilled and shivering, he staggered to his bedroom, wrapped himself in a comforter, collapsed on the bed, and fell into a deep sleep.

When he opened his eyes again, the room was ablaze with daylight. Instinctively, he looked at the clock, which indicated that it was 1:00 in the afternoon. He fully expected Ben to have nudged him awake earlier as part of their regular routine.

"Ben," he called, waving his hand, which was his usual signal for Ben to indicate that he was awake. Then he called out. "Ben, where are you, buddy?"

Soon his memory kicked in, and he remembered what had occurred the day before. Briefly, he felt a surge of confusion followed by moments of sobbing. Tears ran down his cheeks. Reality arrived in waves as the events of the day before resurfaced in his memory. As he slowly regained his rationality, he realized how aberrational his behavior had been, and he struggled to make an effort to stabilize his emotions and restore himself to a saner level of reflection.

After awhile and feeling somewhat more composed, he staggered out of bed and picked up his cell phone that was now fully charged. He noted that there were no recent calls. He pressed Sarah's number and then quickly hung up.

He needed to find some rationale, some way to explain his hurtful rant, knowing that from her point of view, it represented everything she abhorred. Finally, he decided that no explanation would suffice and that any appeal would have to compete with the strength of her emotional attachment to him. If she truly loved him, he reasoned, she would accept some modicum of forgiveness. Wouldn't she? And if not?

After a long period of consideration, he finally called her. The response shocked and confused him. An automated voice told him that the phone number was no longer in service.

"There must be some mistake," he said to the automated voice with rising anger, repeating himself again and again. He began to sense an oncoming wave of depressive loneliness bringing him face to face again with the angst of yesterday.

"Ben!" he shouted into the empty void of his apartment. Then spying Ben's empty water bowl, he wrestled his mind back to reality. Of course Sarah would cut off the phone that had conveyed the hateful diatribe. It was a logical progression. She had removed the offending remarks, lock stock and barrel. He couldn't blame her. He might have reacted in similar fashion, although on further thought, he rejected that notion.

For the rest of the day, he turned it over in his mind, trying to cut through the clutter of his emotions and alight on some course of action. He had determined that he was not going to let her go without a fight, to pursue what he saw as his only path to salvation. Salvation? Now how had that word popped into his mind? Did he mean happiness, contentment, fulfillment? Of one thing he was now dead certain, he needed Sarah to redeem the remainder of his life, and he would discipline himself to give her the breathing space to contemplate how much he truly meant to her.

He had rejected the idea of confronting her immediately. Her anger would be too raw, too unsettled. It was obvious that she had cut off her phone to demonstrate her rage. Of course, he could immediately rush over to her apartment and beg forgiveness, but he rejected that idea out of sheer terror. Not yet, he urged himself.

He tried to calculate how much time she might need to think things through. Surely, he told himself, she would have to reflect on the miracle of their relationship, how joyous it had been, how it had regenerated them in every way, how it had awakened and fulfilled Sarah's sexual longings and reawakened his at a time when he had thought those feelings had been considerably dimmed by age, indifference, and neglect.

She would have to conclude that such a remarkable discovery was surely worth a second chance, however embedded the strength of her tribal loyalty was. In their waning days, when all was said and done, what did ethnic pride matter? In fact, what did anything matter but life, the living of it in bodies that still responded to pleasure, thoughts, imagination and memory? Living trumped everything. Everything! Wasn't it the overriding issue between them as they moved to the finish line? The end. Over. Kaput. Witnessing George die was a revelation of the true meaning of finality.

He would be cautious, he decided, wait it out in the hope that Sarah would cool down enough to rethink her position. He knew he had crossed the line, that her stubborn belief in commitment and loyalty, which had motivated her ironclad pledge to prevent her husband from dying among strangers also applied to her strong sense of identification with Jewish people.

Yes, he would resist the temptation to contact her. She knew his cell phone number and his home address. He would try to keep his life in balance, holding out hope for a swift reunion.

Perhaps, he convinced himself, if and when her anger abated, she would contact him and begin the process of repair. Above all, he feared the disaster of permanent and conclusive rejection. And yet he wondered if such a strategy would negate his long-held idea that words matter, a thought that left him conflicted and uncertain.

Still, deep down, he fantasized that the power of love and

his newly discovered belief in the force of its magnetism would, in the end, prevail. Was he kidding himself? Was he over analyzing, over thinking? Or simply surrendering to some foolish, false, pumped-up illusion about romantic love?

Although he feared both depression and disengagement, he forced himself to find the discipline to sustain his optimism. The idea of being permanently separated from Sarah was too terrible to contemplate, especially now that Ben was gone. He must not let these simultaneous traumas destroy him.

If, after some time elapsed and she didn't call, he would attempt to connect. In the meantime, he decided, he would have to cope with separation and fight off depression and disengagement.

For the next few weeks, he tried to create a livable routine. He immersed himself in details. He took long walks but avoided Central Park. He read the *New York Times* and the *Wall Street Journal* from cover to cover, although he quickly realized that not too much really interested him. He went to the movies, took his meals at various coffee shops, and sat mostly at the counters. He subscribed to Netflix and binged on television series, although few if any of them interested him. He tried rereading old novels that had once attracted him but usually quit after a few chapters.

It seemed that his entire life was totally devoted to listening for Sarah's phone call. It did not come.

At times, he felt he was living through an endless incomprehensible dream. Then, a couple of weeks into this ghostly existence, he decided it was time to take some kind of action. There seemed no point in waiting. He convinced himself that he needed to be proactive and take charge of his life, to engage with people again and try to reconnect with Sarah.

He acknowledged that he was going through the typical

mourning cycle for a lost, deeply missed love. Had he felt this way when Anne died? He couldn't remember.

Then he found the courage to walk to the West Side dog run where he felt certain he would confront his lost lady love. He did this multiple times, always passing her apartment building but unable to bring himself to inquire about her whereabouts. For days he sat on a bench across from the building, waiting to catch sight of her to no avail. Perhaps she was too involved with her husband or on a completely different schedule.

His curiosity became overpowering. At the very least, he assured himself, he was entitled to closure. If it was truly over between him and Sarah, then surely it needed to be resolved one way or another.

By degrees, he felt himself coping, adjusting to circumstances, surrendering to the reality of ending his relationship with Sarah. His walks to Central Park's morning dog runs had sparked his interest in getting another dog. Same breed but older, more in keeping with his own age. He watched the dogs with a jealous eye. He consulted his vet, who said he would keep an eye out for an older Standard.

Still, he was clearly in a state of suspension, as if he were waiting for some inevitable happening that never came. He yearned for Sarah to appear, and as he walked through the park or the city streets, he found himself scrutinizing every person within range, searching for her. There were moments when he actually felt certain that he had identified her from behind, only to discover his mistake at the last moment. More than once he had embarrassed himself by hailing her by name.

When he thought about her, which was most of the time, his recall was tainted by his deep regret about his mad anti-Semitic rant. He could not believe he had done such an awful thing, although as time went on, he felt the price he was paying was far in excess of his crime.

Finally, after a month of agony, loneliness, and an ongoing battle against despair, he conquered his fear of confrontation and the shame it engendered and walked across Central Park to Sarah's apartment building. He felt the full power of his anxiety as he approached the entrance. It was well staffed with two doormen and a man behind the concierge desk.

"Mrs. Silverman, please," he said, feeling his heartbeat accelerate. The young Hispanic man at the desk looked at him curiously.

"She is not in."

Harvey maintained his nonchalance with some effort and nodded.

"When do you expect her?"

"She is away," the young man said. He wore a name tag that identified him as Carlo.

"Away? But her husband was ill."

"He died," Carlo said.

Dead. He felt as if his heart had jumped into his throat.

"Do you know where Mrs. Silverman is?"

"Sorry, we cannot give out that information."

"It is extremely important that I get in touch with her."

"We are not authorized," Carlo reiterated.

"Can you tell me when Mr. Silverman died?"

The young man shrugged. "We have a lot of apartments here. People keep dying."

Harvey turned away, confused and, for a brief time, elated. So it had finally happened, he thought. By the time he returned to his apartment, the irony of it began to assail him. Yet another of God's jokes, he decided, bursting into tears.

-8-

No question about it, Jackson Hole was beautiful, the Tetons were spectacular, and the air of small town living had considerable charm, but it was not Manhattan. Sarah missed the grit, the energy, the electric sense of perpetual movement, and above all, she missed Harvey. But every time she thought about him, her stomach knotted and her rage intensified.

She attempted all kinds of thought games to exonerate him for his disgusting and baffling anti-Semitic outburst but could not reconcile it in her mind. There were moments when her outrage became impossible to quell. Of course, she had heard it all before from others, but it was impossible to believe that Harvey, after all their moments of intimacy and transparency, could have revealed himself as harboring such a horrendous view of her specifically and Jews in general.

In fact, his rant was etched permanently in her mind. After hearing it for the first time, she could not believe it was Harvey. Her first thought was that it was some kind of weird joke. Even when she recounted the circumstances that could prompt such an outburst, she refused to believe it was Harvey.

"You unfeeling Jew whore. How could you not respond? I thought you loved me. You people are all alike. Selfish Jew bastards! You fucking Jewish whore."

Over and over again, it reverberated in her mind. She could not expel it. The words haunted her even now nearly two months after first hearing them. More than once, she tried to rationalize the circumstances. Yes, he was upset. It was understandable. He could not communicate with her. And he needed her, needed her badly to help him through what was clearly an impending traumatic event.

He had no knowledge that she had called 9-1-1 when Frank was having difficulty swallowing and then accompanied him in the ambulance to the Mt. Sinai Hospital emergency department. It seemed alarmingly predictable that Frank's ultimate health crisis would take place during the night when Helena was gone.

How could Harvey have known that Sarah had carelessly left her cell phone at home and was overwhelmed by the circumstances of Frank's agonizing suffering that demanded all her attention? Of course, he would have understood and would have backed away from his own needs. He would want to rush to her side, and nothing would have deterred him.

She had no doubt that her explanation would have calmed him and given him the courage to go through the trauma of Ben's demise without her presence. Yes, considering their relationship, she understood his needs, and she would have gladly found a way to be with him, except for this totally unseen emergency with Frank.

It had been touch and go all night, and Frank's inability to swallow was beginning to affect his breathing. He was gasping for air and struggled through the night until he choked to death. It was beyond frustrating not having her cell phone with her at the hospital, not knowing how to get in touch with her lover.

She did have the cell number for her daughter in Jackson Hole and had called to apprise her of the situation, explaining that she had misplaced her phone. Sheila, as usual, was in some remote place in Africa without a signal. And Harvey's cell phone number was in her misplaced or lost cell phone, and she didn't know it by memory. Nor did she have any doubt that he had tried calling her and had left multiple messages. She had been especially careful to keep the phone charged and with her at all times. It was, after all, her lifeline to both her husband's caretaker and to Harvey.

Helena, who had not been on duty when Frank was having his emergency, was out of reach as well. Thwarted by technology and her own carelessness under the circumstances, she had no doubt that Harvey would completely understand and sympathize with her explanation.

Considering their relationship, she knew, too, that he would be extremely worried, perhaps even panicked. She was clearly guilt-stricken by this perception of Harvey's dilemma. Witnessing Frank's terrible agony fed her guilt, largely because she knew it was an outcome that she had wished for many times over. For this reason, she forced herself to put any thoughts and worries about Harvey on hold while she tried to cope with her husband's suffering. He would surely understand. It was, after all, an outcome for which he had yearned.

She slept in her husband's hospital room all night. He died the morning of the next day. Her initial reaction was relief, which only fed her guilt until rationalization kicked in. She had kept her word, had fulfilled her promise through his ordeal, and stood by his side until the very last moment of his life. On balance, she told herself, she had fulfilled the marriage pledge—in sickness and in health. Thankfully, she could still recall the memories of their long and essentially happy marriage.

Frank had chosen years ago to be cremated, and of course, she had no reason to counter his instructions. By then, Helena had arrived and taken charge of the arrangements.

"God has asked for him," she had intoned.

When Sarah finally arrived back in her apartment, she was totally exhausted and immediately fell into a deep, exhaustive sleep, a kind of mental collapse that wiped away all consciousness.

Upon awakening, she discovered her missing cell phone under the comforter of her bed. It needed to be charged. Once it was plugged in, she listened to Harvey's desperate messages. She was about to call him when she heard his last recording. She was stunned.

She replayed it a second time, then a third, totally confused by its tenor. It triggered an accelerating rage. She flung the phone against the wall, disabling it completely.

What galled her most was that she had not detected even the barest hint of such hateful thoughts in their early days. Yes, she told herself, he was facing the loss of a much devoted companion. Yes, she could understand his need to have her at his side during the traumatic moment of Ben's death. She, too, was attached to Shaina and knew the difficulties of being present at such an event. She had left Shaina in the doorman's charge with instructions to have her walked and fed by one of the many dog walkers that served the building's tenants.

Dealing with Frank's death and Harvey's monstrous rant had its effect. Grief and disillusionment did not go well together. She could barely deal with her own rage. How could she not have detected this in what she had come to believe was a joyous, utterly transparent, and miraculously compatible and passionate late-life relationship?

There was no way to disguise her depressed and brooding state. Both her daughters had interpreted her condition as mourning for her dead husband, which was only partially true. The twin episodes of death and disillusionment left her deeply depressed, unable to focus, and determined to immediately eliminate Harvey from her life. Her first act was to sever all communications. She purchased a new phone with a new number.

Her daughter Charleen and Helena were the only attendees at Frank's funeral at the crematory. It was Sarah's choice. She wanted no clues for Harvey.

Charleen, seeing the terrible state of her mother and attributing it to the trauma of Frank's death, suggested that Sarah come to Jackson Hole for a few months to, as she put it, "chill out." Sarah jumped at the chance without hesitation.

There was no point staying in New York. She had written Harvey off as a companion with whom to live out the years she had left. It was not solely because of the blatancy of his hidden anti-Semitism, it was the secrecy of his bias, the horror of his internal harboring of such hateful thoughts and the fear of living forever under a smoking volcano of hatred.

Actually, as time passed, she felt herself lucky to be rescued from the fate of living with the stress of knowing how he felt about her and Jews in general. *A Jew whore.* The words bounced around in her mind like a pinball, banging up against any hope of transparency or sharing. How could he have talked about love? When turning it over again and again in her mind, she would often feel a growing physical nausea, and for many days, she was unable to eat.

Living in close proximity to Charleen's lifestyle choice had its own challenges to Sarah's comfort level. It had troubled her at first, this conscious rejection of traditional family life, complete with husband and wife conceiving children and all the legacy matters they entailed. There were now established paths to simulate such a relationship, and her basic live-and-let-live liberal instincts induced total acceptance.

Charleen, or Charley as she wanted to be called, lived in a renovated small log cabin with a spectacular view of the Grand Tetons. Her partner was a woman about 10 years younger, very feminine in her ways. Her name was Dolly, which pretty well described her persona. As Sarah observed the relationship, her daughter seemed to play the male role. Teaching skiing in the winters and horse wrangling at a nearby dude ranch in the summers had given her a tough muscular fit, far more masculine than she appeared in her formative years living at home. Dolly worked as a waitress in town, and the atmosphere in their home was compatible and loving.

Both were caring and considerate, dedicated to helping Sarah repair her psyche, although they did not know the real root cause of her problem since she kept that to herself. She did manage to take long walks on the lower mountain trails, and the exercise, the climate, and the rough beauty of the area helped somewhat.

It took her some time to discover that her sudden diminishment of energy that had been charged up by New York City was like air going out of a balloon. Now, where there had been action and noise, there was silence, dead silence.

There were sounds, of course, but they were of the occasional jet plane overhead or the natural noises made by animals at night, particularly coyotes or wolves, and during the day by cattle and horses. Another welcome surprise was the vast array of stars that lit up the sky on a clear night. It offered the eternal message that in the scheme of things, she was an inconsequential speck of life on a small planet in an infinite universe. Such insight made her concerns seem petty, trivial, and frivolous.

In what she termed a classic irony, Shaina collapsed on one of their walks and died, and Charley and Dolly ceremonially buried the dog in their backyard and topped it with a wooden marker. She was, of course, sorely missed by Sarah, although she did not experience the emotional turmoil that had jolted Harvey.

The truth of it was that she felt uprooted and alien. The Western ethic was light years away from West Side New York, a ground zero for liberals, especially Jews. Most of the people she met casually in Jackson Hole hated all politicians, distrusted government, and were conservatives.

They pulled any voting lever that wasn't labeled Democrat. Charley's circle was not among the *nouveau riche* who were descending on the town, mostly to escape state and estate taxes and fantasize about Western values, Western dress, Western cuisine. And of course, there were the ski slopes and the invasion of the super wealthy and their plethora of winter and summer toys.

"It used to be different," Dolly told her. She had come from Salt Lake City from a large Mormon family who now considered her a "jack Mormon," or renegade. Oh, there were the usual rich dudes who came up here from the East Coast and West Coast for the Western experience, but mostly, this was a place for ordinary people, working stiffs, cowboys, and rancher types whose grandparents had homesteaded their land and really loved the place. Now, the rich guys were taking over, and everything had changed. And not for the better.

"Only they can't change the mountains and the environment," Charley had offered up like a Greek chorus of historical analysis.

For Sarah, her concerns revolved more around the age issue, specifically her own. There was no avoiding the looming threat of the approach of the grim reaper. So far, she had been blessed with robust health and physical durability. But she couldn't ignore the aches and pains of approaching infirmity. Her energy was flagging. She needed extended afternoon naptimes. Food was less tempting. Distance was challenging the length of her walking, and she was feeling the muscular strain and diminishing lung capacity.

The few people that Charley tried to involve her with remarked on how well she looked for her age. She was pushing 82, and it was a sop to her vanity to be told that she could pass for the late 60s. Who was she kidding? She was a fucking old lady, heading toward the ultimate endgame.

All her life, in every situation, she had been gregarious,

eager for conversation and communication. In her new environment, she grew less talkative, more insular and silent, which prompted Charley to interpret her conduct as a bout of severe depression. She suggested seeing a doctor, which Sarah refused.

"I just don't feel much like mixing," she countered.

"You need people, Mom," Charley would advise.

"I have people. You and Dolly."

"I mean people your own age. Besides, we work all day."

"I'm fine," she would protest. "I'm adjusting."

"And I'm worried."

"I'm not."

Of course she was depressed, but she had no desire to see a doctor who might prescribe happy pills that would dull her senses. Her experience with Frank made her wary of anything that might react on her brain, concluding that if she was truly depressed, a healthy brain would eventually restore her mental equilibrium. Of all the afflictions that might attack her, she feared loss of mental clarity and memory the most.

Her acute self-awareness diagnosed her present state as depressive brought on by anger, disillusionment, loneliness, and lack of purpose. She missed Frank, despite his diminished mental state. She missed Helena and her discipline. She missed her apartment, its collection of varied possessions collected in her long married life. She missed her doormen, the art-nauseous lobby of her apartment building, the elevator that sped her to her corridor. She missed the hustle and bustle and energy of New York City. She missed its noise, its crowds, and its smells. She missed the traffic, her super-charged advocacy, the clash of opinions. She missed its many contrarian voices, the tall buildings, the way the city lit up at night, the restaurants, the choices, the charging hordes, the clop clop of the horse carriages around the park, the dog runs, the dirt, the smog, the entertainment, the risks, and, dammit to hell, Harvey.

Sometimes when she heard the sound of the coyote baying in the black night, she imagined it was her voice, screaming into the void. But by morning, her insight kicked in, and she felt a sense of temporary rescue as if she were clinging to flotsam in an infinite ocean, wondering if rescue would ever arrive in time.

Nevertheless, she knew, too, that she was blessed with an odd compensation, a long-term memory of extraordinary power and clarity. It had become a place of refuge, and she would spend many conscious waking hours recalling the events of her life, the names and faces of people with whom she interacted, and the highlights of such interactions. She could remember most of the details of her early days living with her parents and could vividly recall bits and pieces of memory from infant days to now, a gift akin to a miracle with deep emotional resonance that often felt like movie music beats.

Although to Charley and Dolly she might have appeared like she was living in the moment, she spent most of her time recalling the images, sounds, smells, and feelings of waves and waves of incidents of a life lived. Digging deeply into her memory, she recalled old addresses, old telephone numbers, the names and faces of cousins, teachers, friends, lovers, music, movies, neighborhoods, food, street sounds, smells, voices, celebrations, embarrassments, arguments, gaffes, mistakes, deaths, funerals, impressions, aspirations failed or fulfilled, and sexual experiences, the full gamut specific and uncensored with males, females, old, and young.

There was the historical content as well, the background noises of wars, religion, politics, the agony of others, the striving to do good, adding her voice and deeds to make the world kind and comfortable for every human being on earth. And the inexplicable hatred against those birds of a different feather, blacks and brown and yellows, especially the Jews who had been condemned, murdered, tortured, exploited, and driven from place to place. She hadn't always felt the tribal connection, but hatred had a way of uniting the hated, and she had succumbed to that sense of belonging and become a mortal enemy of those who blindly despised her tribe.

Yes, she decided, such a passionate sense of belonging seemed to create some possessive gene that expressed profound unity and defensiveness against the carrier of what was, in her mind, an opposite gene, the hate gene.

Still, the emotional logic on such subjects began to pale as one grew closer to the end, meaning the end of memory, which meant the end of living. Was there a lesson in this, some truth that was eluding her? What really mattered as one approached the finish line? Was there an ultimate truth?

It occurred to her that only the very old, like her, with the gift of long-term memories could relive the events and circumstances of a life lived and with luck and persistence find the truth of it. Could one find this illusive truth in the totality, the sum total of what living meant, the doing of it, breath after breath, heartbeat after heartbeat? L'Chaim, she would say out loud, sometimes repetitively, usually on a lone walk at sunrise when the world looked new and orange.

Actually, she remembered sharing this gift with Harvey, who was equally blessed with vivid long-term memory, and in their limited time together, they had offered each other living memoirs of their lives. When she recalled these conversations, she marveled briefly but was invariably cut short by her anger and accusations that he had deliberately censored such memories as revealed by his hateful rant.

Clearly, from her daughter's point of view, she carried an age number that pigeonholed her into the perception of being a super senior, an irrelevant old fart to be tolerated, entertained, amused, and palliated by well meaning do-gooders. Good God, she detested the breed who saw no difference except by number.

What you son of a bitches don't know is that I've got a shitload of wisdom bouncing around in my brain about which you haven't got a fucking clue, she railed at those she imagined had designated her as stale leftovers to be tossed in the old-age trash heap.

There were attempts by Charley to get her involved with Jackson Hole's older set and the various services provided by the town for retirees, most of them former ranchers, bartenders, storekeepers, cowboys, and housewives, the traditional group of Wyoming old-timers. Although they were colorful and decent people, they had lived lives so different from hers that any attempt to mix with them only added to her isolation.

Occasionally, she heard remarks that indicated a mindset not unlike the hidden bias that had bubbled to the surface in Harvey's rant, but she reacted silently, realizing that it was part and parcel of the culture where people were used to such common statements as "jewing down," "pushy kikes," or "they own all the media and secretly run the government." Fuck them. They were hardly worth the energy of rebuttal.

Jews were not part of Charley's circle, and the years of Hebrew school and Jewish holidays observed during her formative years seemed to have happened to someone else. Not to mention that Charley had changed her name from Silverman to Silver and was contemplating marriage with Dolly, whose last name was McCarthy.

Her wandering save-the-world daughter, who was sent to Hebrew school as well, had probably long rejected any notion of Jewishness, or so she speculated. She loved them, of course. Wasn't she supposed to? In her heart of hearts, she was often guilt-ridden by the possibility that Frank and she had been too accepting of their whims and wanderings. The truth was that they had moved far, far away from any original parental aspirations. *Do your own thing* was a family mantra, and that's exactly what they did.

There were not many Jews in the area, and although that population was on the rise, she oddly did not bond with them. Perhaps she resented their obvious efforts to fit in, to find tribal anonymity in this mostly alien turf.

There were, of course, people of her political persuasion among them, but for some reason, she felt no kinship with them. There was no synagogue in town, and for the Jewish holidays, observant Jews went to Boise or Salt Lake City or elsewhere, and there was an occasional service in the basement of the local Episcopal church. She made it her business to attend these events, if only to show her tribal affiliation.

As part and parcel of her so-called internal living memoir, she devoted time revisiting her early wilder days, her life with Frank, her days as a mother of little girls, and her passionate days of political activism. Although she tried, she could not totally close the door on her affair with Harvey, the good moments, the playful moments, and especially the sexual moments. Unfortunately, they were always accompanied by a long chain of bitter invectives.

Her sense of suspended animation continued along with a deep self-appraisal that had only occurred in her bonding conversations with Harvey. She had been more open with him than with anyone else in her life and had laid it all out for him, soup to nuts, her inner life, her fears, her insecurities, her relationship with her husband, the joys and consequences of her early life. Every time she thought about these revelations, she felt sick to her stomach. How could she not have known the real truth about how he felt about her—the Jewish whore?

Another odd thing had occurred. She no longer felt any

sexual urges. It both astonished and saddened her. She tried to summon interest, manipulated herself with her private toys, and summoned up fantasies that had once induced a surge of sexual feeling that had always been reliable precursors of orgasms. No longer.

What a mess, she would tell herself when she inspected her body in a full-length mirror. Her tits, the pride and glory of her womanhood, were beginning to look like low-hanging sacks. Her belly appeared bloated, and if she inspected herself with her reading glasses, the veins along her arms and legs seemed more pronounced. Looking over her shoulder revealed drooping ass cheeks. There was now no mistaking her physical body for anything more than that of just an old broad. Self deprecating humor somehow seemed to lighten the sharp blows of reality.

Inspecting her face, especially in the bright daylight of the high altitude, told her the truth about the nooks, crannies, and wrinkles that loosely fitted the contours of her face. She was one old biddy, although remarkably, she was still physically fit, which indicated the payoff of good genes and years of exercise and movement. What it told her was that she was accepting the fate of life's ending.

She had put her apartment up for sale and was in touch with the broker, who was getting lots of bites in what was a rising real estate market in Manhattan. After paying off her mortgages obtained to finance Frank's illness, she should net enough to carry her through a simplified life, depending on where she settled for her final days. Yes, at her age, she had to think about final days. Neither daughter seemed to care about their inheritance, if any. Charley had little financial demands. Expenses for her and Dolly were at a minimum, and the issue did not seem to be a concern.

Sarah was not used to being in a kind of limbo and had no desire to make new friends, which was probably a reaction to what had transpired with Harvey and what now was associated in her mind as a massive betrayal.

One day in mid-June as she walked along a flat trail near Charley's cabin, she heard the unmistakable barking of a dog. Each bark ended in a kind of dog whine that, she knew from her experience with Shaina, was the sound of a dog in pain. Following the sound, she discovered a dog of uncertain breed caught on some barbed wire fencing strung along the borders of the ranch that abutted an area not far from Charley's cabin.

Sarah approached the dog cautiously, and after managing to placate it, gently extracted it from the barbed wire. The dog, a male, seemed sickly and had no collar or identification.

"Now what?" she said, addressing the dog who had curled up to lick the wound made by the barbs. She kneeled beside him and stroked his coat, which was badly in need of a bath. He smelled bad, and no amount of licking could close the gashes made by the barbs.

Having been a loving dog owner, she could not leave the dog to suffer alone. The wounds needed dressing, and while the dog carried no identification, she knew it was not an uncommon sight to see uncollared dogs roaming about that belonged to people who were not prone to follow the rules. She spent time stroking the dog to gain his confidence, and finally the dog stood up. It seemed like he did not want to leave her.

"Go home, buddy. Hell, you got here. You must know the way back."

The dog stood up but seemed shaky, and she noted that one leg seemed injured. When the dog did move, he maneuvered himself on three legs. Although he was scrawny, he was too heavy for her to carry. She was not far from the cabin and could see its outlines in the distance.

At first, she tried to coax the dog to follow, but he seemed too uncertain and probably scared to follow her signals. She decided to remove the leather belt that secured her slacks, loop it around the dog's neck and very gently urge him to follow her. It took some time to win his confidence, but walking on three legs, he followed her back to the cabin.

Charley had taken her pickup truck and Dolly her car, leaving Sarah with no transportation. She hadn't felt the need to have her own wheels, and when it was feasible, she could borrow either vehicle while the girls made other arrangements, which was not often. Back at the cabin, she washed and dressed the dog's wounds, inspected his leg, which did not seem broken. A thorn was caught in his paw, which she removed with tweezers.

Using Dolly's scented soap, Sarah worked hard to remove the dirt that had accumulated on his coat. He seemed to accept her ministrations, after which she put him out to dry in the sun and scooped up some leftover meatloaf onto a plate. Then she filled a soup bowl with water. He made quick work of both offerings.

Assessing him, she tried to identify his breed, but then accepted the notion that he was obviously a mutt. After the dog took what seemed like a much-needed nap, Sarah assumed it would mosey back from whence he had come. Only he didn't—or wouldn't—budge.

While Charley and Dolly liked animals, their busy lifestyles did not allow the time or responsibility for a pet. The next day, Dolly and Sarah took the dog to the nearest vet where they had him checked out.

"He's a mix alright. Part lab. Part poodle. Probably part fox terrier. But who knows. I'd say he was about six or seven. Not fixed."

"So what am I supposed to do with him?" she asked.

"Three choices," the vet told her. "Put an ad in the local paper with the dog's description and hope someone answers it. Lots of strays and abandoned dogs around these parts. The fancies coming to live here, usually look for a purebred. But out here, dogs adopt people and just hang out with whoever feeds them or who they get attached to. Some get mauled by moose, run over by cars, or killed by predators. Some get picked up by good Samaritans like you. You can, if you choose, bring him to the pound. Or you can leave him with me, and I'll get them to pick him up. If no one claims him, he'll be put down. Or, third option, keep him. With care, he should be in reasonably good shape in a few weeks. I'll see that he gets a license." The vet winked. "Your call, lady. I can give him the shots he needs and put him on the right nutrition. He's no beauty, but he seems like a good sort. Maybe he just got kicked out or his old master died. Who knows?"

He lifted the dog's snout and looked into his eyes.

"You a good sort, buddy?" The vet turned to Sarah and inspected her as if he had read her thoughts. "Take him home. Put an ad in the paper, and see if you get any bites."

She did exactly that. But after a couple of weeks with no bites, both Charley and Dolly urged her to keep him. At first, Sarah tested a long list of names on him, hoping for recognition. None worked, and she finally decided to call him L'Chaim.

"That's ridiculous, Mom," Charley admonished.

"La what?" Dolly asked, giggling.

"Means 'to life' in Yiddish," Sarah explained, remembering her conversation with Harvey.

"Like Shaina meant pretty," Dolly said, remembering the translation.

L'Chaim became Sarah's constant companion, accompanied her on her daily walks, and slept at the foot of her bed. She was happy that no one had claimed him and that he had not wandered off to find another master or mistress. She patiently trained him to heel and obey the rudimentary commands of "sit" and "stay," and he soon grew familiar with his name. Her care and feeding brought his weight up, and visits to the vet assured her that he was getting along fine.

"He is one ugly sight," Charley would opine, and by the usual standards, Sarah acknowledged that she was spot on. His gait was clumsy, his coat was a washed-out brown like stale chocolate, his underbody sagged, and his snout was flat and did not quite fit his overall look. His saving grace was his eyes, deep brown and full of curiosity and energy.

He had an odd habit of staring at Sarah for long periods, especially when she held his stare with her own, as if they were in silent communication. She spoke to him often, especially when their eyes were locked together in a fixed gaze.

"What the hell are you looking at?" she would ask him often. "What you see is what you get, an old broad with a long story waiting for what comes next."

He was a terrible watchdog and would sleep through all interruptive noises, barking only when he wanted attention from Sarah, which was often.

On their daily walks, Sarah kept him leashed but then unleashed him in large spaces with good visibility. It became apparent to her one day that she was training him for city life. The fact was that she still was unsure where to plant herself for the rest of her life. She had received offers for her condo but was procrastinating, not on the issue of price but largely because she could not face the enormous effort of sorting through possessions, making decisions on what to keep and what to reject, and unsure about any future plans.

A woman alone, healthy for her age, and certain that she was still viable mentally and physically, she did not feel comfortable with her own age group. Perhaps she was lying to herself or simply being snobbish and, heavens to Betsy, elitist, but she could not shake a sense of isolation. The irony of her situation was that despite the simmering rage she felt about Harvey, whenever the memory of their so-called affair surfaced in her mind, she could not escape the fact of their bonding, of being on the same wavelength, of being compatible and happy together.

Neither Charley nor Dolly had a clue about her plight. To them, she was probably characterized as an old lady who needed companionship, patience, and understanding, or whatever bromides were traditionally prescribed for people in their 80s. They did not have a clue about the curse of her being called out as typical of the 80s being the new 60s.

With her new buddy L'Chaim at her side, devoted, unquestioning, and, above all, a good listener, she was able to offer a steady stream of pithy dialogue, yes dialogue, meaning the ugly son of a bitch was taking it all in and offering answers in dog body language, an idea that made her hysterical with laughter.

"So what's your advice, buddy?" she would reiterate again and again as they walked along the nearby trails around the cabin. "Stay or go? What the fuck would you know about a Jimmy Durante routine? Or even Lassie, for that matter, or Rin Tin Tin. How the hell did you get stuck with an old biddy who once thought the West Side of Manhattan was the whole fucking world?" L'Chaim would look up at her and wag his tail, which seemed to belong to another breed. "Now tell me true, L'Chaim, would you be happy to come back with me to the Big Apple and live in close quarters with no more than a daily dose of freedom in Central Park with all those pampered purebreds and their entitled fancy owners?"

She rarely passed another human being on her walks, which had become a daily routine, even in rough weather. She felt certain that if she did, they would think she was either senile or possibly talking on her cell phone.

In late summer, she felt the need to return to New York. She imagined she felt whole again and ready to face the real world, although she remained tentative about her permanent venue.

"You seemed happy here," Charley said after she announced she was heading back to New York.

"You and Dolly have been great, but there are loose ends to take care of. I want to follow through on a potential condo sale and get myself organized. I'll be fine. Then I'll decide where to plant myself." She looked down at L'Chaim, who locked into her eyes. "See? The mutt agrees."

Charley knew better than to attempt to dissuade her mother from doing something after her mind was made up. It was clearly apparent to both mother and daughter that Sarah was perfectly capable of administering her life. Her years as an attorney had honed her skills for organization, and both agreed that her cognition was remarkably acute for someone of her advanced years.

"I just hope I have your genes, Mom," Charley mused frequently. As for her Sarah's physical agility, Charley marveled at her mother's health and stamina. "Maybe you can get yourself a boyfriend."

"Who the hell would want a wreck like me?"

"You fishing for compliments, Mom?"

"Or maybe a girlfriend," Charley suggested, winking at Dolly.

"Find me a nice shiksa like Dolly, and I might get motivated."

Planning for her return to New York, Sarah was determined to keep herself busy. She had finally decided to take the best offer and sell her condo, a fairly complicated process that was bound to take two or three months, depending on the acceptance of the new buyer by the condo board, which was getting pickier these days. Considering the costs associated with Frank's long illness, she figured that if she got a decent price, she could maintain a comfortable lifestyle for herself as long as her health permitted.

It did require considerable mental adjustment to confront her new circumstances. There were so many details to arrange, including the very painful chore of choosing what needed to be disposed of in her effort to downsize. She hadn't fully made up her mind about whether or not she would go back to Jackson Hole or stay in New York, a decision she would keep in abeyance as she readjusted to life in the city.

But she did enjoy reconnecting with the New York beat, and while she had not yet attended any of the various cultural events playing at Lincoln Center and the plays and musicals on Broadway, she did see the various art movies being shown at Lincoln Plaza. She had missed the daily *New York Times* that she had subscribed to for decades and quickly renewed her home delivery subscription. By reading it, she felt more plugged in to her old life. Besides, it reflected her liberal bias, which was not true of the local papers in Jackson Hole.

Thankfully, the many details that had to be dealt with kept her focused on pressing practical matters. She did make vague plans about pursuing her various advocacy causes and reviving her social and organizational contacts. Unfortunately, she discovered that her long lapse from such connections caused by supervising Frank's last days and her intense affair with Harvey had pretty much taken up all her time. Many of her usual contacts in advocacy organizations had dried up in the interim. Nevertheless, she was determined to join the fray again.

Helping L'Chaim adjust to his new life was another consideration. It took him awhile to reclaim his recent housebroken habits, and keeping him leashed at all times when outdoors took further adjustment. She did walk him along the periphery of Central Park, which might have reminded him of his carefree Wyoming days, but she did not feel ready to revisit the morning dog runs, fearful that old memories of her affair with Harvey would resurface, feed her nostalgia, and recall her rage. It was something she felt she must wipe out of her memory bank.

She did renew her relationship with her old doctors who had served her for many years. Her internist pronounced her reasonably fit, except for slightly elevated blood pressure, an increase in cholesterol, and some signs of arthritis of the spine, which was attributed to the aging process and did not interfere with her mobility. Her blood work was fairly normal, and the doctor predicted that she could, with luck, look ahead to another decade.

Her former gynecologist had died, and she found another one, much younger and in her early 30s who examined her nether parts and ordered breast cancer tests. The results indicated that she was in excellent condition for her age. When it came to the question of whether or not she was sexually active in her widowhood, Sarah felt the urge for a naughty response.

"Will the equipment sustain a hard cock?"

The doctor laughed and nodded, saying, "I see no reason why not."

"I used to masturbate a lot, but I seem to have lost my fervent desire."

"Sometimes it takes time to reassert itself after a husband's death."

Actually, she knew the comment was far off the mark and offered a subtle correction. "I had a lover," Sarah exclaimed, adding, "during my husband's illness."

"What happened to him?"

"Good question," Sarah said, nodding. "Actually, he was older than me. We had a lot of sex."

"Did he die?"

She hesitated a long time before answering, sorry she had brought up the subject. Oddly, the question troubled her. Harvey dead? She felt a sudden sensation of loss. For some reason, she avoided the answer, and the doctor ignored the omission.

"From my limited experience, older women are still sensual and react to stimulation. My field is the physical, not the psychological. But if you feel the need, find a partner. "

"Got any ideas?" Sarah asked.

"Sorry, I only treat women."

"Worth a try," Sarah chuckled, thinking of Charley.

Perhaps the doctor's advice to find a new partner made sense. To that end, Sarah made some effort to shave some years off her appearance by dying her grey curly hair black and allowing a makeup person at Bergdorf's to, as she put it, give her a more youthful look. On the advice of the makeup artist, she was persuaded to buy clothes in lighter colors that would add to the illusion of her being younger.

The redo got raves from the doorman but made her feel synthetic and phony, although she thought it might lure some unsuspecting swain to think she was, say, in her late 60s or maybe early 70s.

Telling possible partners that she was pushing eighty three was not exactly an inducement for a romantic engagement, although her age had not deterred Harvey who had the looks and build to attract a younger woman. He had fallen for her without the camouflage of dyed hair and a painted face. Oddly, the memory of their clandestine affair was beginning to recycle in her thoughts, albeit with a declining sense of rage, although his anti-Semitic outburst still rankled and confused her. At times, she actually thought it was not his voice on her phone, an idea that she knew was more wish fulfillment than fact. Still, she continued to erase the experience from her memory with increasingly diminished results.

Indeed, she began to wonder why he did not attempt to find her, but then it was she who disappeared from view, escaping secretly to Jackson Hole, deliberately covering her tracks. Obviously, Harvey either had no detective skills or had meant what he said, knowing he was throwing her under the bus.

On the other hand, he might have decided not to pursue the Jew bitch whore image that had surfaced in his mind. Of course, even if he did find her, she would have told him to go fuck himself and never darken her doorway again. Hadn't she imagined such confrontations in the days of her exile? Besides, how could he possibly explain the outburst to her?

By the beginning of September, she had sold her condo and was waiting for the condo committee to approve the new owners, a couple in their late 20s, one of the newly minted millionaires of the startup generation.

Often, she would subject L'Chaim to comments and observations about her life, noting that he would continue to maintain eye contact as if he truly understood what she was staying.

"Even though my husband Frank was out of it, I do miss him. In fact, I miss caring for him, however difficult it was. All in all, we had a great life together."

Finally, armed with her new look, she began to take L'Chaim to the dog runs on the West Side. By then, her latent fear of meeting Harvey again had dissipated, although she wondered often whether she was secretly hoping to run into him, if only to show him how little he now meant to her.

L'Chaim seemed to enjoy his new freedom gamboling with the other dogs, most of them with identifiable pedigrees, although they seemed non-discriminatory when L'Chaim tried to mount them. Most, however, had been fixed and not very interested, although some of the parents raised their objections to Sarah.

One disgruntled parent, a wiseacre bearded character in a Yankees baseball hat, rudely expressed himself to Sarah.

"You should really get that ugly mutt castrated. Imagine what will come out of coupling with him."

At first she ignored the man, who was a regular and persisted in taunting her whenever she arrived for the morning routine.

"I keep trying to picture the result," he would remark and shake his head when observing L'Chaim's occasional conduct.

"Just look in the mirror, buddy. You'll get a preview," Sarah shot back.

He did not comment again.

Although she did not solicit the friendship of the other dog parents, she did feel subjected to more attention from the various older men who watched their dogs from the sidelines. Perhaps she was merely imagining such a reaction or subliminally recalling the attention Harvey paid her at their early interactions.

Toward the end of September, about the same time she had originally met Harvey at the East Side dog run, she decided to grant herself an anniversary present, which is the way she characterized the effort. She could not deny the impact of her memories about their affair, although the residue of her rage continued to simmer.

She spent most of her time going through the accumulation of possessions that she and Frank had acquired during their long marriage. The process of downsizing was daunting. Frank's clothes had to be disposed of. There were piles of photographs, books, artwork, and files connected with her former law practice and Frank's teaching and research projects. The apartment was stuffed with what she now termed memorabilia, the storage and disposal of which taxed her organizational skills.

Then there was the question of where she would move. She had determined not to buy but to rent, which required her to search for apartments that took pets. The upside of these activities was that it filled her time and left her little time to feel sorry for herself.

And she did have L'Chaim, who was now the principal live being that shared her life. She pampered and groomed him, although no amount of physical attention could do much about his odd appearance. In her mind, he became a symbol of diversity, a coming together of disparate entities to create a single compatible and loving, living whole. This characterization fitted well with her staunch progressive views.

"You're the proof, kiddo," she would tell him often, rubbing his head. "You are the most beautiful, ugly son of a bitch in the world." Oddly, he would bark his response, which she would interpret as a happy comment on his part.

Finally, she made the long Hegira to the East Side dog run. With pounding heart, she approached the site of their first meeting. There was absolutely no logic in her quest since she knew that Ben was gone, but she harbored the wild notion that his attachment to him would have induced him to replace him, as L'Chaim had replaced Shaina. But hadn't that been pure coincidence? Or fate? Being mostly alone could induce such irrational ideas.

Of course, she knew exactly where he lived. Hadn't she once stood near the entrance to the park waiting for him and Ben to arrive? Perhaps such an irrational action on her part was the first stage of oncoming dementia. Having lived through the horror of such progression in Frank, she was not immune to speculation that it could happen to her, despite the present accuracy of both her long-term and short-term memory.

Hell, she thought, she could remember the details of her third birthday party and every element of her life up to now, including every tiny act and conversation between her and Harvey, including all the deliciously raunchy parts, right up to the ugly memory of his anti-Semitic rant.

She released L'Chaim on the dog run, asking herself what the fuck she was doing here. She scoped the terrain and the dog parents, and to what she termed her relief, she saw no one who resembled her once lover. She had begun the walk from the West Side when it was still dark, the sun rising as she walked.

Her Jackson Hole stay and her long walks along the low Teton trails had physically strengthened her, and she arrived at the area just as the other parents arrived. L'Chaim did his usual sniffing, running and occasional humping, eliciting oddly aggressive thoughts and whispered expressions. "Fuck these East Side shits, L'Chaim. Show them what balls we West Siders are blessed with."

She was so absorbed in her rant that she didn't hear it at first. Then she did.

"Boobala!" the voice cried. She knew immediately who it belonged to, and she felt certain that her heart missed a beat. Then she saw, of all things, a chocolate standard poodle looking up and staring at Harvey. He was dressed in exactly the same clothes she had last seen him in, and remarkably he looked as if he hadn't aged one bit.

Boobala ran to his parent, who bent down to pat him for a moment and then let him wander back to the pack, one of who was L'Chaim, who was showing interest in the poodle, who was apparently a female. There was a moment, even from that distance, that their gaze locked, and Sarah could see Harvey squint and briefly turn away.

It's me, you Jew-baiting bastard, she told herself, although her heartbeat had accelerated now. Her knees felt weak as she watched him turn back to look at her, confused but obviously engaged. Then it was her turn to look away, as if she hadn't noticed him. She held her breath. Was he coming toward her?

What she hadn't realized at first was that she had redone herself. Her hair was black. She had carefully put on her makeup, which she had never done before in the morning, and her clothes were a far cry from what she wore when they first met.

"I'm sorry if I stared," he said, his voice coming from behind her. "You remind me of someone." She could sense him standing behind her, obviously confused and uncertain. "I guess I made a mistake."

Finally, she turned. She did not smile, her teeth clenched, her face flushed.

"Yes, it's me, Harvey, you fucking Jew-baiting shit."

Their eyes locked. He flushed a deep red. "I dreaded this moment, Sarah. It was unforgivable."

"Nor will I ever forgive it."

"I don't know where it came from."

"From you, Harvey. It came from the words matter guy."

"Yes, it did. I wanted to cut off my tongue." His eyes teared up, and he turned away.

"Believe me, Harvey, I don't feel your pain."

"How was I to know about Frank?" he said, sucking in a deep breath.

"Frank was dying. I misplaced my phone." She paused. "Why am I explaining this?"

Their eyes locked again, and he blew out his breath.

"Ben was about to die. I needed you." He swallowed his words, and tears brimmed and ran down his cheeks. "I...I loved you both," he began, and then could not continue. She watched him. He had turned ashen and struggled to speak. "I love you, Sarah. I always will. We were a miracle."

"It proved my point, Harvey. In the end, they curse the Jews."

"I'm not they. "

They were silent for a few moments, then both turned simultaneously to watch their dogs.

"Which is yours, Sarah?" His voice quivered slightly.

"The ugly one," Sarah said.

"Not ugly. Just different. What's his name?"

She felt a lump grow in her throat as she hesitated.

"L'Chaim."

"To life," he whispered. "Nothing else matters."

He turned toward her and smiled. Again, their eyes locked.

"I heard what you named yours, Harvey."

He made no comment, lost in thought.

"Will you be here tomorrow? Or is it West Side?" asked Harvey.

"Might be gone by tomorrow, Harvey. But I do know where I am today. And I sure could use a glass of Champagne."

"Boobala!" Harvey screamed. The dog turned and ambled forward.

"L'Chaim!" she called, and he obediently ran up to be leashed.

"I've got two bottles waiting in the fridge," he said, reaching out to grab her hand.

"I think I saw this movie, Harvey," Sarah said as they moved onto Fifth Avenue.

About the Author

Acclaimed author, playwright, poet, and essayist **Warren Adler** is best known for *The War of the Roses,* his masterpiece fictionalization of a macabre divorce adapted into the BAFTA- and Golden Globe–nominated hit film starring Danny DeVito, Michael Douglas, and Kathleen Turner.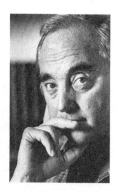

Adler has also optioned and sold film rights for a number of his works, including *Random Hearts* (starring Harrison Ford and Kristen Scott Thomas) and *The Sunset Gang* (produced by Linda Lavin for PBS's American Playhouse series starring Jerry Stiller, Uta Hagen, Harold Gould, and Doris Roberts), which garnered Doris Roberts an Emmy nomination for Best Supporting Actress in a Miniseries. In recent development is the Broadway production of *The War of the Roses* as well as a number of film adaptations in development with Grey Eagle Films including *The Children of the Roses, Target Churchill, Residue, Mourning Glory,* and *Capitol Crimes,* a television series based on his Fiona Fitzgerald mystery series. Find out more details about all film/TV developments at www.Greyeaglefilms.com

Adler's works have been translated into more than 25 languages, including his staged version of *The War of the Roses,* which has opened to spectacular reviews worldwide. Adler has taught creative writing seminars at New York University, and has lectured on creative writing, film and television adaptation, and electronic publishing. He lives with his wife, Sunny, a former magazine editor, in Manhattan.

For complete catalogue including novels, plays, and short stories visit: *www.warrenadler.com*

Did you enjoy LAST CALL? Then please leave a review on any of the below retail websites:
Amazon.com
Goodreads.com
Barnesandnoble.com

Connect with Warren Adler on:
Facebook—www.facebook.com/warrenadler
Twitter—www.twitter.com/warrenadler
BookBub—www.bookbub.com/authors/warren-adler